SASQUATCH HUNTERS ❶

The SASQUATCH
of HAWTHORNE ELEMENTARY

KB Jackson

By K.B. Jackson

REYCRAFT
BOOKS

Reycraft Books
55 Fifth Avenue
New York, NY 10003

reycraftbooks.com

Reycraft Books is a trade imprint and trademark of Newmark Learning, LLC.

Text © 2023 by K.B. Jackson

All rights reserved. No portion of this book may be reproduced, stored in a retrieval system, or transmitted in any form or by any means, electronic, mechanical, photocopying, recording, or otherwise, without written permission from the publisher. For information regarding permission, please contact info@reycraftbooks.com.

Educators and Librarians: Our books may be purchased in bulk for promotional, educational, or business use. Please contact sales@reycraftbooks.com.

This is a work of fiction. Names, characters, places, dialogue, and incidents described either are the product of the author's imagination or are used fictitiously. Any resemblance to actual persons, living or dead, is entirely coincidental.

Sale of this book without a front cover or jacket may be unauthorized. If this book is coverless, it may have been reported to the publisher as "unsold or destroyed" and may have deprived the author and publisher of payment.

Library of Congress Control Number: 2022906758

Hardcover ISBN: 978-1-4788-6852-1
Paperback ISBN: 978-1-4788-7965-7

Jacket and cover illustration by Lorenzo Conti

Photo Credits: Title Page A, Page 12A, 21A, 29A, 43A, 53A, 63A, 77A, 90A, 105A,114A, 121A, 132A, 139A, 150A, 156A, 163A, 172A, 181A, 193A, 200A: andreashofmann7777/Shutterstock; Title Page B, Page 1B, 12B, 21B, 29B, 42B, 53B, 63B, 77B, 90B, 105B, 114B, 121B, 132B, 139B, 150B, 156B, 163B, 172B, 181B, 193B, 200B: mirjanajovic/Getty Images; Title Page C: A-Digit/ Getty Images; Page IV, Page 1A: A-Digit/Getty Images
Author photo: Dioncia Von Bargen-Miles@ Natural Approach Photography

Printed in Dongguan, China. 8557/0722/19331
10 9 8 7 6 5 4 3 2 1

First Edition published by Reycraft Books 2023.

Reycraft Books and Newmark Learning, LLC, support diversity and the First Amendment, and celebrate the right to read.

CONTENTS

Off on the
Wrong (Big)Foot

I stood lurking around the tetherball pole when she approached me.

"Hey."

"Hey." I attempted to appear casual by shoving my hands in the front pockets of my jeans. It was difficult to be nonchalant with fidgety fingers.

"Word on the street is you're the one I should see about…" She glanced around and lowered her voice. "Something I saw."

I scanned the playground to see if anyone was within

earshot. They weren't. Redirecting my gaze back to the girl, I was surprised to see that she looked as nervous as I felt.

I'd had many conversations just like this one, but never with anyone quite so pretty. Her blue eyes sparkled with intrigue but were slanted with concern. Experience had taught me to be cautious in my response. These requests weren't always as they appeared.

"Hello?" Her tone was clipped and impatient. Her mouth, slathered in sticky lip gloss, twisted into a nervous scowl.

"Who told you to come talk to me?" I felt suspicious of her motives but wanted to believe it wasn't a setup.

She scrunched her Tinker Bell nose and narrowed her eyes. "If you're gonna be such a pain, maybe you aren't the one I should be asking for help."

With that, she turned on her heel. TOMS, it said.

"Wait."

She turned just enough to glance over her shoulder.

"Tell me what you think you saw."

Her face grew flushed and her expression went from annoyed to angry in an instant. She came at me quickly until we were standing nose to forehead.

For clarification: her nose, my forehead.

"Listen, you little twerp. I don't *think* I saw something. I *know* I saw something."

Her warm Fruity Pebbles-scented breath blew onto my face. Fruity Pebbles were my favorite. I stepped back, trying not to smile. It was hard to take an angry person seriously when they smelled like sugared berries.

"Okay, tell me what you saw."

She glanced around again. "Not here. Can you meet me at the park across the street after school?"

"Yeah, I'll be at the climbing rock."

She nodded and turned again to walk away.

I called after her. "Wait. What's your name?"

"Jasmine." She flounced her long, wavy strawberry blonde hair over her shoulder and did a half-skip, half-jog back to a group of girls watching an intense game of wall ball.

I observed the game from a distance, as I did most recesses. Michael Blackwell and his right-hand thug Charlie Jones appeared to be retaining their titles as the kings of wall ball against two fifth-grade boys.

Michael's dad was a county sheriff's deputy,

a fact I'd learned on my first day at Hawthorne Elementary School.

Allow me to back up a moment. My name is Jake Q. Nelson. Don't bother asking what the Q stands for, because I'll never tell. I turned twelve last August, two days before my mom and I relocated from Orlando to Hawthorne, Washington.

Leaving my life in Florida, saying goodbye to my best friend Chase, and moving to the farthest reaches of the United States—aka the Pacific Northwest—was hard enough. Starting the first day of sixth grade with no friends was harder. Getting on the bad side of the most intimidating kid in my grade within two minutes of setting foot off the bus simply sucked. Big time.

I confess, I hadn't been watching where I was going. Michael couldn't have been looking, either, or the collision wouldn't have happened, but he'd never admit it.

I'd felt the bump before I saw him, as I'd been looking at my book, *Tristan Nance Has a Secret* by Alfred Higbee.

I'd read all of Mr. Higbee's other books, my favorite being *Did Jed Wooden Just Locate the Lost City of Atlantis*? However, as amazing as Jed Wooden was,

Tristan Nance was a character I could relate to. He'd experienced some bad luck and some loss, and had to rely on himself to survive. That's how I'd lived my life since arriving in Washington—in survival mode.

In the book, Tristan's world is changed forever when he finds his mother's diary, which reveals his father was the god Apollo. I dreamed of the day when I might meet my father, hoping he wasn't some jerk who'd abandoned my mom and me but someone I'd be proud to call Dad. I had no illusions he'd be a superhero, but someone who'd take me to a baseball game or teach me how to shave was better than nothing.

I was sure he had a good reason for not being in my life. I just didn't know what it was yet.

The only thing I knew about my father? My mom once told me he was "a big man, in more ways than one." I'd found that difficult to believe, considering I was nearly a head shorter than every other kid in my class. I figured maybe she meant he was fat. I didn't have an ounce of fat on me, so I must have inherited all my mother's genes.

Anyway, back to my fateful run-in with Michael Blackwell. I'd been reading the Tristan Nance book when suddenly my face was surrounded by what I later realized was the bulk of Michael's expensive ski jacket.

He'd made some sort of squawking sound, and then something hit the ground. I didn't even have to unbury my face from his jacket to know what that noise meant. Something had broken, and it sounded expensive.

"Hey!" he'd screamed, pushing me away.

I stared at the shattered remains of a smartphone.

"You broke my phone! I just got it for my birthday!"

"I...I'm so sorry. I didn't mean to. It was an accident." I took a step backward.

"I don't care if it was an accident! You broke my phone, and now you have to buy me a new one."

I didn't have a cell phone and had no idea how much a fancy new one cost, but I did know it was more than I had in my safe. Forty-six dollars and eighty-seven cents, to be exact. I looked around. A crowd had begun to gather. The hairs on my neck raised, and my Spidey-senses told me I was in danger of getting punched in the mouth. His face had turned the color of the icky stewed-tomato casserole my mother makes. Not good—his mood nor the casserole.

"My father works in the county sheriff's office! If you don't pay for me to get a new phone, I'm gonna have him arrest you." He practically jumped up and down in fury.

"Is that legal?" squeaked a tiny voice to my left.

I looked over. A small boy, who couldn't have been more than a third grader judging by the fact that I towered over him, stood there with his eyebrows pulled together in deep concern.

"Shut up, Lanny. No one asked you!" The irate phone owner bellowed at the boy, causing him to shrink back into the crowd.

"Look," I attempted to reason with him the way my mom had taught me to resolve conflict. She'd told me I'd be in big trouble if I got into any fights. "I'm sure we can figure something out."

"Oh, we're gonna figure something out, all right." He stepped closer and loomed over me.

I looked at him and saw he had a booger in his left nostril. I decided it would be unwise at that moment to enlighten him about that fact.

"You're gonna buy me a brand-new phone. Maybe even an upgrade."

At this point, one of the adults with a badge and a whistle, who'd been directing kids coming off the buses, made her way over to the gathered crowd.

"Everything okay here, boys?" Her tone implied she knew it wasn't. "Michael, what happened?"

I assumed she was talking to the other boy. Michael. Now I knew the name of the kid I wanted to avoid from then on.

"He bumped into me and knocked my brand-new phone onto the ground, and it shattered! And now he says he's not gonna pay for it!" The boy whined, which made him seem slightly less intimidating. Only slightly, though.

The woman turned to look at me. She reminded me of Mrs. Langford, our next-door neighbor in Orlando. She had the same white hair with the same short haircut. She wasn't smiling at that moment, but her golden eyes were surrounded by smile wrinkles, so I had the feeling she might be an ally. I really needed an ally about then.

"I didn't say I wouldn't pay. I just said it was an accident." I had no idea how I would pay or if it were even my responsibility, but my hope was a little cooperation would help get her on my side.

Her gaze softened a bit. "What's your name, honey?"

"Jake. Jake Nelson."

"You're new here, aren't you?" Her voice held a kindness that made me feel safe.

"Yeah—uh, yes, ma'am. My mom and I just moved here from Florida."

"I think we should go into Mrs. Farnsworth's office and sort this whole thing out. You two boys follow me. The rest of you, get to class!" She made a shooing motion.

The crowd began to disperse, and I heard snatches of conversations. I'd been unable to determine the bulk of what they were saying, but I knew they were talking about me judging by the words "Florida," "short," and "dead meat." I also thought I caught a "kinda cute" but was too embarrassed by the whole incident to get a look at who might have said it. So much for flying under the radar.

Michael and I had followed the white-haired lady up the steps and into the main office. I'd been in there two weeks prior when my mother had registered me for school.

The secretary glanced up from what she'd been doing as we walked in.

She greeted the white-haired lady. "Already? The first bell hasn't rung yet!"

"Just a little misunderstanding," the Mrs. Langford look-alike sang.

I liked her more by the minute.

I later learned her real name was Ms. Hinkle. Not Mrs. Hinkle, but Ms. Hinkle. She was very particular about that.

She led Michael and me into the large room in the corner of the office, which held nothing more than a long table, a few chairs, and a plant. A closer inspection of the plant revealed it to be fake, and clearly it hadn't been dusted in a while.

"Okay, boys, have a seat. Mrs. Farnsworth will be in here to talk to you in just a moment."

I watched her leave and then looked over at Michael. His face looked smug.

"My dad comes to the school once a month to do D.O.N.T. He and Mrs. Farnsworth are like this!" He crossed his fingers and shoved them into my face.

At the time, I had no idea what D.O.N.T. was, but one thing I knew for certain. If Michael's dad and the principal were tight, the situation wasn't in my favor.

I later learned D.O.N.T. was our school's version of D.A.R.E. (Drug Abuse Resistance Education) The initials stood for "Do Only Nice Things." They were both programs that brought local law enforcement officers into schools to try and keep kids from getting into trouble, but apparently Mrs. Farnsworth didn't want the officers to talk about serious trouble and wanted to keep things a little more rainbows and sunshine.

She'd say things like, "When your friends ask you to do something you know you shouldn't, D.O.N.T.!" Sometimes she'd end her morning announcements by saying, "Don't forget D.O.N.T.! Make good choices," which I found to be very confusing.

Michael's declaration about his father having an in with the principal made my stomach drop. I'd backed up and dragged a chair toward me, plopping myself down with a sigh. Michael pulled out the leather swivel chair from the head of the conference table and sat. He leaned back and gave me some serious stink eye.

I'd made an enemy before my first day had even begun.

The Client

I plowed my way through the rush of kids streaming from their classrooms just after the end-of-school bell rang. Backpacks swung wildly. I nearly got my eye poked out dodging all the umbrellas popping open. Moms called their children's names from within their cars parked in what we called the kiss-and-go lane.

My mother claimed it was more like the yell-and-not-move-forward-when-you're-supposed-to lane.

"Thank goodness for buses," she'd said one day after picking me up for a dentist appointment, blowing a strand of her long, dark hair from her face in frustration.

"I think if I had to deal with the parents in this line twice a day, I'd end up doing something we'd all regret."

I stepped out from under the eaves and joined the stream headed for the crosswalk. There was a light drizzle, but I'd learned pretty quickly in Seattle that a little rain never kept people from doing stuff.

In Orlando, my Little League games got called for less dampness than this, but the weather there was usually either sunshine or hurricane. No one knew what to do with the in-between.

I crossed the street with a group of rambunctious kids and their weary parents, who'd been talked into going to the park. The parents found spots at the picnic tables on the covered patio while their children ran off in multiple directions. Little girls jumped onto the swings, a bunch of fourth graders headed for the zip line, and about ten boys began picking teams on the grassy area for a game of touch football.

I witnessed this scene nearly every day as my bus drove by the park after school, so when my bus passed—with Lanny looking longingly out the window at the scene below—just a few minutes later, I knew how he felt.

I had a plan to meet with Jasmine and then walk

home. I wasn't exactly sure how far it was, but I believed I knew the way, and it seemed doable. My mom wouldn't even notice if I was later than normal since she didn't get home until dinnertime.

I leaned against the climbing rock and waited.

"Look out below!" A voice screamed from above me.

A body whooshed over my head, landing at my feet.

"You're crazy! You could have landed on me!" I yelled.

I knew even before she looked at me that it was Jasmine because of her long, reddish-blonde hair, which reminded me of my grandfather's dog Butch, a golden retriever/collie/Irish setter mix. I'd never tell Jasmine because she might get the wrong idea and think it was an insult. It wasn't. Butch was one of the prettiest dogs I'd ever seen, and Jasmine was one of the prettiest girls I'd ever seen.

In my opinion, Butch was the worst name for a dog with flowing golden hair. A dog that pretty—even a boy dog—should be named something like Goldie or Sampson.

Jasmine laughed. "I saw you. I just wanted to scare you a bit." She stood and brushed wood chips from her jeans.

"So, are you gonna tell me why we're here?" I demanded. "What did you see that has you so freaked out?"

"Come with me." She began walking toward the corner of the park. She didn't stop to make sure I was following, I guess because she was used to people doing what she said. She strode with confidence straight through the middle of the football game, bringing it to a screeching halt. Michael stood holding the football, observing us with a glare.

"Hey, Jasmine, whatcha doin'?" Michael sneered at me.

In what I would come to eventually recognize as a nervous tic, Jasmine flipped her long, blonde hair over her shoulder and casually called out, "None of your beeswax, Michael."

Charlie, who stood at Michael's side like the good little minion he was, whispered loudly enough for everyone to hear, "Michael, are you gonna let her talk to you like that?"

Michael's face looked a bit like the first time I'd met him, a reddish-purplish color that reminded me of an angry cartoon character. The only thing missing was steam coming from his ears. "Jasmine, if you wanna hang around losers, go ahead. But you know what hanging around losers makes you?"

She whipped her whole body to face him, her long mane flying behind like a superhero cape in the wind. "Well, Michael, whatever it makes me, I already was, since I've been hanging around you since preschool!"

It took every ounce of self-discipline I possessed not to leap in the air pumping my fist and yell, "Oh yeah!" Instead, I tucked my chin and averted my gaze so Michael wouldn't see me smirking. I took off behind her as she stomped the rest of the way across the field.

Behind us, the boys playing football gave Michael a hard time about being put in his place by a girl. Unfortunately, I knew Michael was a grudge-holder. He'd get back at us somehow.

Jasmine led me to the edge of the park. I'd never noticed the clearing in the trees or the path through the laurel bushes and rhododendrons. I hadn't really ever thought about what was on the other side of the park.

"Have you been here?" Jasmine whispered excitedly.

I peered into the wooded area. Beyond the shrubs, it looked shaded and a little dark. "Nope. What's back there?"

"Well, the path goes pretty far into the woods. There have been a lot of rumors about homeless people living in there, bank robbers hiding out, and kids having parties. Some say there's a doorknob high on a big tree where elves come and go."

"Have you ever been back there?" I tried not to let my nerves show.

Of course, the idea of elves living in a tree, like the cookie makers from the commercials, was ridiculous. Then again, most people thought the idea of a giant ape-man roaming the forests of the world was ridiculous as well, but I knew it to be true. Once I accepted the premise that there were things in this world which couldn't be explained by current conventional wisdom and scientific theory, I'd opened my mind to all sorts of possibilities.

"Yes, that's why you're here. Two weeks ago, I had a sleepover at Kayla Kim's house. Do you know Kayla?"

"Kayla is the tall Chinese girl, right?"

Her face scrunched, and she gave me a condescending stare. "She's not Chinese. She's Korean."

"Oh, sorry."

"Anyway, Kayla and I snuck out of her house at

about eleven that night. We met here with a couple of other friends who'd snuck out. We'd all made a bet that whoever could stay back here in the dark the longest won."

"Won what?"

"That's not the point," she huffed.

"Why won't you tell me?" My curiosity was getting the best of me.

"You don't need to know that." She declared the subject closed with the crossing of her arms across her chest and the pinching of her mouth.

"Whatever. So, what happened?"

"Kayla went in first. She lasted like sixty seconds before she came flying out. Danielle was next. She made it maybe two minutes. Erika saw the looks on their faces and decided she wasn't going in, so she quit the bet. I went last."

Her face changed as she talked, like watching a thunderstorm roll in. Her breathing became more rapid, her eyes darkened, and her lips quivered.

"I walked in, and it got darker with every step. I kept spooking myself whenever I stepped on a branch. The leaves were rustling on the bushes on both sides of me.

My heart felt like it might explode—it was beating so fast, but the competitive side of me kicked in, and I wasn't about to give in yet." Her gaze darted around as she told her story.

I must admit, my own heart started to beat a little faster listening to her.

"A little way in, I came to a large tree. It looked like it had an opening at the base of the trunk someone might be able to crawl into. There was a tarp tied to one of the branches and some garbage on the ground. I could tell someone had been staying there, or at least hanging out there. I stopped and looked around, but I didn't see anyone. The strangest part was all the noises I'd been hearing completely went quiet. There wasn't a bird chirp, not a squirrel in the trees. Even the bushes seemed to freeze motionless in suspended animation. There wasn't a single sound. It was eerie." Her voice had hushed to a whisper, and her eyes began to well up with liquid as if she were going to cry.

Oh, please don't cry, I thought to myself.

"I need you to promise me something." Her shaky voice became demanding.

"What?"

"Lanny told me you have…experience with…strange

happenings. I need to know you'll listen to what I have to say and not make fun of me. And I need to know you won't tell a soul. No one." Her eyes were round as saucers, barely containing the tears that threatened to spill out all over her face.

"I promise." And I meant it. I knew what it was like to tell a story and have no one believe you.

She took a deep breath. "I think…no, I'm pretty sure…almost positive…I saw," she hesitated and then spat out the word. "Bigfoot."

The Bigfoot Theory

My eyes widened to match Jasmine's. "What...what did you see?"

"I sensed him before I saw him. My body started tingling, and I got goosebumps all over. I felt torn between curiosity and the fear of what I might see. I slowly turned around, and through the trees I saw the outline of a man, only he was bigger than any man I'd ever seen before. I was using a night vision app on my phone, so I couldn't really see his face. His eyes though, they glowed. Like my cat's eyes."

By this point, all my senses were on high alert. "What color?"

"His eyes? Kind of yellowish-gold. Like I said, they looked like my cat when it's looking through the sliding back door at night."

"Maybe it was a cat on a tall branch."

Judging by her expression, she didn't like that suggestion. "It was not a cat. These eyes were too far apart to be a cat. Besides, how would you explain the shadow of a giant figure?"

"Okay. So, what did you do? What did *it* do?"

"I froze. It stared at me. And I stared back. I heard it breathing, and it smelled like one of those portable toilets they have at the soccer fields. My throat felt like it was closing. It reminded me of the time I ate mango and found out I was allergic. I couldn't scream if I wanted to, and my legs felt paralyzed. Suddenly, a rock came flying and landed right next to me. It must have unfrozen my feet because, before I knew it, I was running as fast as I could back over the trail. I didn't slow down until I was completely out of the woods and with my friends."

"How did they react when you told them?" I studied her face, and everything in me believed her. She'd seen something which had scared her half to death.

She blinked at me and then looked down at her silver sparkly shoe as it dug a small hole in the dirt. "I didn't."

"How come?"

She looked at me again, her eyes filled with worry and embarrassment. "I couldn't. I knew they wouldn't believe me, and they would make fun of me."

"But they're your friends."

Her laughter sounded bitter. "Just because they're my friends doesn't mean if I tell them some crazy story, they won't tell the whole school. I'd become the laughingstock of the world!"

I knew what she meant. I'd learned early on that some things were not well received by the public in general, and kids could be cruel. I'd had firsthand experience. People I'd thought were my friends had not only been embarrassed to associate with me after they heard my story, they had joined in on the teasing.

"So, what did Lanny tell you about me?"

"Lanny's my little brother's best friend. The Monday after this happened, he came home from school with Josh. They walked in on me Google searching for Bigfoot sightings in Washington. Josh made some jokes about me smelling like a Sasquatch. When he left to go to the bathroom, Lanny told me anything I wanted to know about Bigfoot, I should ask you."

Lanny has a big mouth, I thought to myself.

A few weeks earlier, I'd been sitting on the bus working on my journal when Lanny popped his head over the seat in front of me. I knew him as the little kid who'd challenged the legality of Michael's claim that he could have his father arrest me for his broken phone. I'd seen him on the bus, but we'd never talked.

"Whatcha doin'?"

"Writing in my journal." I pulled it closer to keep it private.

"What are you writing about?" He either didn't notice or chose to ignore my annoyed expression.

"Observations." My abrupt tone did nothing to curb Lanny's curiosity.

"What kind of observations?" His big brown eyes grew even larger than normal. "Like a spy?"

I let out a frustrated sigh. "Field observations."

"I don't know what that is." He looked at me expectantly.

Reluctantly, I flopped the journal upside down onto my lap. "I go out into the woods near my grandfather's house every weekend and take notes on what I see, what I hear, and what I smell."

"What you smell? What are you smelling for?" He wrinkled his nose.

"Uh, animal smells." I didn't want to give him any more information than I already had. I'd been down this road before. Questions led to more questions, which led to even more questions and ended with me being made fun of. I was determined not to make the same mistakes I'd made at my old school.

"You're weird," Lanny declared, tilting his head to the side as he appraised me. It didn't quite sound like an insult. It almost seemed like a statement of approval.

I blinked at him. "So are you."

"I'm not weird. I'm smart. I'm in Hi-cap, highly capable." He said this with great pride.

"Same thing."

My mom had wanted to sign me up for the advanced Hi-cap class, but, believing it would make my social life even more difficult, I'd dug in my heels. I'd been struggling to fit in with the popular kids. Heck, I'd even been struggling to fit in with the unpopular kids.

"So, are you looking for wild animals? I saw a coyote behind my house last summer."

"Sort of."

"Can I come with you?"

"Where?"

"To the woods. My parents say I spend too much time on the computer, so I have to spend every Saturday outside. Usually, I wander my neighborhood until I find a friend who'll invite me in to play video games on their computer or TV. When I come home for dinner, my mom makes me write an essay on what I did that day. Usually, I make it up, so you'd be doing me a favor if you let me come with you." He punctuated this with a hopeful toothy smile. "That way, I could write about real adventures, not fake ones."

"Your parents make you write essays?" It was a horrifying concept. Homework on top of homework.

"We're Indian," Lanny said, shrugging his shoulders as if this were a complete explanation.

"So?"

"My mom says it's the job of Indian parents to make sure their kids will be successful in life. My dad wants me to be a lawyer like he is. My mom would rather I be a doctor. There are a lot of doctors in my family. My mother says, 'No one becomes a doctor playing Minecraft all day.'" He'd mimicked a woman's high-pitched and chastising voice. "I tried to build a Minecraft hospital to prove her wrong, but she just rolled her eyes and grounded me for the rest of the evening."

"Your parents are strict."

"Yeah. But they say they have to be because I'm so... pre...precourse? precorsus?"

"I think you mean precocious."

"Yes, precocious. So, can I come?" Those big brown eyes looked at me with enthusiasm, and I wondered how he ever got in trouble with that face.

I thought about it for a minute before deciding it might be nice to have someone with me on my expeditions. "All right. You can come with me. But this is a confidential expedition. Do you know what *confidential* means?" I asked this with all the scowling seriousness I could muster. He needed to know I meant it.

"Of course. It means it's a secret. Like a spy."

"Yes. No one is to know what we're doing or what we

see. Do you understand?" I maintained my stern tone and expression. "I have to know I can trust you not to leak this information."

His eyes sparkled with even more excitement. "Yes, sir!" And then he did some sort of salute.

"What was that?" I chuckled.

His cheeks turned pink. "I don't know, it just felt right in the moment."

I guess I could have been mad at Lanny for telling Jasmine, but if he hadn't, I never would have found myself standing next to a pretty girl with an amazing story who was looking at me to help her solve the mystery of what she'd seen in the woods behind Hawthorne Park.

Skunk Ape Jake

As I walked home from the park following my meeting with Jasmine, it occurred to me there was a big difference between riding the bus and walking. I was fifteen minutes in and still had a long way to go. My legs were tired, but my mind raced. What Jasmine had described sounded very similar to the story my grandfather had told me two summers prior, the story which had started me on my crazy quest.

Before I'd left the park, I'd taken a quick peek into the woods without going in too far. I'd looked around but didn't see or hear anything unusual. Even more important, in my mind at least, was the fact I hadn't smelled anything unusual or skunky, only wet trees and dirt.

I'd told Jasmine I would do some online research about the area, take some notes, process my thoughts, and get back to her with my analysis.

"Do you have a card or something?" she'd asked before we'd left the park.

"A card?" My forehead wrinkled.

"A business card. You know, with your phone number, email, the name of your company." She sounded impatient, as if she thought I was intentionally being evasive.

"My company?" I asked, confused.

"Lanny says you're the president, and he's the vice president."

I laughed. "Lanny is delusional."

"If you're gonna be a famous Bigfoot hunter, you probably should come up with a name for your company. Also, you should print business cards to give out to people." She put her hand on her left hip with attitude.

"I'm not trying to be famous. I'm just trying to prove it exists."

"Do you really think if you prove Bigfoot exists, you won't become famous?" she asked. "It would be the discovery of the century! Maybe the whole history of the world!"

I had a lot of time on my hour-long walk home to think about what she'd said. I wasn't necessarily doing it to become famous, but maybe if I did become famous, my dad would read about me and come find me.

My mom never talked about him. She hadn't told me I couldn't ask questions about him, but every time we watched a show together with a dad playing catch with his son or taking him fishing, she would look at me with a sad expression, as if she felt bad for me. I hadn't wanted to make her feel worse, so for the most part I'd left the topic alone. With her, at least. It didn't mean I'd stopped fantasizing about the day we'd meet or that I hadn't done a little internet sleuthing on my school laptop to see if I could figure out who he was. I'd had no luck.

He probably didn't even know we'd moved to Washington. I determined right then and there I was going to become the most famous Bigfoot hunter ever. Jasmine was right. I needed business cards.

When I got home, I ran to my room and pulled out

my journal. I found a blank page and began designing my business card.

Sasquatch Hunters
of Washington, Inc.

Jake Q. Nelson
President and CEO

I thought about adding a phone number, but I didn't have a cell phone, and the last thing I wanted was my mom answering the phone when someone called asking for the Bigfoot hunter. It wasn't that she couldn't afford to buy me a cell phone, but my mom worked in tech, and she'd decided it was in my best interest that I didn't get one until junior high school. She was always ranting about cyberbullying and kids losing their attention span because of swiping and scrolling all day. I had a school laptop, but I wasn't allowed to use it for anything other than schoolwork. She also wasn't exactly supportive of Bigfooting as a hobby and rolled her eyes every time my grandfather and I talked about Bigfoot shows, or he showed me new videos of sightings posted online.

When my mom told me she was thinking about moving us from Florida to Washington to live with my grandfather, I wasn't happy. Besides leaving the only home I'd ever known, I didn't know my grandfather very well. The only times I'd seen him were during a couple of visits we'd made to Washington for Christmas, and the summer I'd turned seven, when he'd come to Florida to take me to Disney World.

That's where my mom had worked, Disney World, and why she'd moved to Florida in the first place. She'd dropped out of college, packed her stuff, driven across the country from Seattle to Orlando, and applied for a job at the theme park the next day. She'd had a dream to play a princess. She liked to say, "You don't choose the princess life. The princess life chooses you."

Unfortunately, she couldn't just walk into the role of a princess—she had to work her way up. For the first several years she paid her dues as one of Snow White's dwarfs, and, if she got lucky and someone called in sick, one of the ugly stepsisters from Cinderella.

About four years after she'd started working at the theme park, she got pregnant with me. She often laughed about it these days, but at the time, having to pull off a giant dwarf head to puke every morning couldn't have been very fun. When I was born, she'd taken a little time off to take care of me and get back into princess-ready shape. Five years after arriving in Florida, she finally made her princess debut, proudly sitting upon an orange shell throne in Ariel's Grotto.

Eventually, though, she'd tired of the princess life and moved over to corporate headquarters for an administrative job as an executive assistant. She'd said she missed seeing the smiles on all the little girls' and boys' faces as they shyly approached her for a hug and an autograph, but being a mom meant making choices based on financial security, not dreams and fairy tales.

She said being a single mom was tough, and expensive, and sometimes lonely. She rarely dated, and while I knew she loved spending time with me, I knew deep down she wished she had someone to love—a grown-up, manly someone—and to share the burdens of life. I felt bad about the fact I was one of them. I never wanted to be a burden to my mom.

One day, she announced she'd applied for a position at Amazon, and we were moving to Washington. My grandfather offered to help us relocate and to have us stay with him until my mom got settled in at her new job.

No one ever asked my opinion on the matter. It's not

like my life in Florida was perfect. It definitely wasn't, but it was the life I knew.

Mom seemed happier in Washington and a lot less stressed, which did make me happy, but I knew she worried about whether I was making friends, because every night when she got home from work, she asked who I sat with at lunch and if I wanted to invite anyone over. No lie, moving and starting a new school wasn't the easiest thing I'd ever gone through in my life, but I was surviving.

I will say, getting to know my grandfather better was the best part of moving. He'd grown up on the Olympic Peninsula near Port Angeles, home of the Elwha Klallam Tribe, and he was an old-school kind of guy. He liked fishing and hiking and building things with his own hands.

How someone like him had a daughter like my mother was beyond me, because they couldn't have been more different. My grandfather was solid. Stable. Steady. Calm. My mother...was not. She was a pie-in-the-sky, head-in-the-clouds sort of person. She always believed things would work out. My grandfather called her impulsive and impractical. She said she just believed in herself and the people around her.

I hadn't ever had the nerve to ask if my father had betrayed her unwavering faith in her fellow man, and if that's why he wasn't in my life. I often wondered, though, what he could have done that had been so bad I couldn't know him.

• • •

After I finished making my first business card, I got to work researching Sasquatch sightings in the area. No one had ever reported seeing anything in the woods behind the park, but that didn't mean there wasn't something there which hadn't yet been officially discovered.

"Jake? Are you home?" My grandfather tapped on my bedroom door.

"Yeah, Gramps."

He opened the door and peeked his head inside my room. "I didn't see you get off the bus today. I got a little concerned. Everything all right?"

"I walked home." I hoped he wouldn't pry too much.

A look of surprise crossed his face. "You did? How come? Did you miss the bus?"

I fidgeted with my backpack's zipper. "I had a

meeting, an appointment with a client. My first client, as a matter of fact."

He opened the door wider, came into the room, and sat at my desk. He looked around at my stuff strewn all over the floor but said nothing about it. Gramps was the kind of guy who didn't need to say a whole lot, or anything at all, really, in order to make his feelings known. I'd be sure to clean my room that night.

I took his silence to mean he was waiting for an explanation.

"I've decided to start my own business." I announced this with more fanfare and bravado than I felt, nervous about how he would respond.

"I see. What sort of business?"

I blew out a breath. "A squatch-hunting business." I handed him the paper business card I'd just made.

He studied the card, and I held my breath, worried he might tell me I couldn't do it.

"So, you say you've got your first client, huh?"

"Yes." I felt proud and grown-up.

"A paying client?"

"Uh." I hadn't thought about asking for money for

my services. I'd been too busy thinking about getting famous. "We haven't discussed my fee yet. She just hired me today."

"She?" His left eyebrow, gray and bushy, popped up in surprise like an old groundhog predicting the weather.

"Her name is Jasmine. She's in my grade but not in my class." I paused before continuing excitedly. "Gramps, she says she saw a Bigfoot. By the school!"

My grandfather leaned back in the chair and it groaned its disapproval. "Jake, are you sure she's not just messing with you?"

"You sure do ask a lot of questions."

"I'm trying to understand, and perhaps in the process, some things will become clear to both of us. Now, about this girl, how do you know she's not playing a prank?"

I tried not to let his skepticism temper my enthusiasm. "I thought about that at first when she approached me. After everything that happened back in Orlando…" I trailed off. "But her face, I don't think she could be that good of an actress. She saw something, and it really freaked her out."

My grandfather sat thinking, as he was prone to do. He didn't react right away like my mom usually did. Sometimes I wondered if she were adopted.

"Do you want to tell me about her experience?" His voice had a calming effect, like the slow rhythmic creak of his rocking chair and the warm spice of the pipe he smoked every evening on the porch. He gave the impression he had no place he'd rather be than right there with me, for as long as it took.

And so, I relayed every bit of information I could remember Jasmine had told me. When I'd finished, a huge whoosh of air left my lungs. "That's it. That's her story."

"And quite a story it is," he agreed. "Over by the school, you say?"

"Yes, there's a path into the woods from the edge of the park."

He rubbed his chin pensively. "It's sort of hard to imagine something so large and unusual could go undetected so close to a busy school and park."

"But no one goes back there!"

I felt exasperated. He, of all people, should have been more understanding.

"Hey now, take it down a notch. I'm just helping you look at other potential explanations. The key to a good investigation is to not go into it with a predetermined outcome in mind. You need to write out all the possibilities of what she could have seen, and then eliminate them as the evidence reveals itself."

Deep down, I knew he was right, but it felt like he'd thrown a wet blanket on my fire.

"Gramps, you know something could be out there because you've seen it with your own two eyes. I wish you would tell your story, and share what happened. People know you and trust you as someone who tells the truth."

"Which is exactly why I will never tell anyone. I have a good reputation in this community, and there's no way I'm risking it on some story I can't prove. I'm not going down as Crazy Old Man Nelson when my story is written."

I understood why he felt the way he did, even though I didn't like what he was saying.

I'd learned that lesson the hard way when I'd returned to Florida for the first day of fifth grade after spending the summer in Washington and began regaling my classmates with tales of my grandfather's encounter with a beast of mythic proportions. I'd ended up in the principal's office that day. There'd been a bit of a scuffle at recess after Mickey Carter had called me a liar. Socially, I'd never lived it down. From that day on, I'd been known in several circles as "Skunk Ape Jake."

I hoped I wasn't setting myself up for Skunk Ape Jake: the sequel.

Eagle Eye Nelson

I'd spent the summer between fourth and fifth grade at my grandfather's place. At the time, my mom was transitioning to her new position in the corporate office, and the training had been intense.

She'd sold it to me as having the choice between the lesser of two undesirables: ten-hour days at Mrs. Langford's condo, which smelled like Vicks VapoRub, with her super slow internet and basic cable, or two months helping my grandfather take care of his five-acre property about an hour north of Seattle. The weary look on my mother's face told me the latter would be best for her. Besides, I'd been promised a few camping trips, and I'd never been camping before.

The first couple of weeks after I'd arrived in Washington, I'd learned to drive Gramps's riding lawnmower, mend fences, chop wood for the firepit, and fish. During the day I didn't really have time to miss my mom but at night, exhausted from the day, I often laid my head on my pillow, and the ache for her was overwhelming. My muscles hurt too, sore from all the work I was doing, but it was nothing compared to the way my heart had hurt.

I'd never experienced the feeling of missing someone before. Not like that, anyway. I'd sometimes had similar sensations when I woke from dreams about meeting my father, but that was more a dull, distant feeling I didn't quite know how to identify. It was harder to miss what I'd never known.

After my third week in Washington, Gramps had decided it was time to get me out into the woods. He'd sensed I'd started to crack under the weight of missing my mom and figured a change of scenery would do me good. We woke early one morning and packed the old blue van with all the supplies we'd need. He'd hooked up his aluminum boat trailer, and I got a little nervous about taking it into the deep, dark, and cold Pacific waters. Then he threw a large crate into the back.

"What's that?"

"It's a crab pot." He'd answered this as if I should know.

"A crab pot? Like for catching crabs?"

I knew once I'd said it, it was a silly question. My grandfather, however, didn't mock me.

"Yep. You drop it off the side of the boat. When you pull it back up, hopefully there are crabs inside." He hoisted a large white Igloo chest into the van.

"I've never had crab."

That stopped him in his tracks.

"You're kidding."

"Nope. Mom doesn't like seafood, remember?"

"Well, boy, I'm about to introduce you to what is sure to become one of your favorite foods."

"What if I don't like it either? Maybe I'm allergic. Mom says she's allergic."

"She's not allergic; she's just picky. Do you like butter?"

"Of course!"

"Well, then you'll like the way I serve crab. I drench it in butter."

I'd decided to reserve judgment, even though, in my mind, I figured anything which required being smothered in butter to taste good probably didn't taste good.

We drove about forty-five minutes from Gramps's house to the ferry dock. Since it was early and we were crossing Puget Sound toward the Olympic Peninsula, the line wasn't very long. Cars streamed off the ferry one by one until soon our line began to move, and the cars ahead of us drove onto the boat. Finally, our turn came.

I'd never been on a ferry boat before. It was kind of like driving into a tunnel. Or a cave.

The day was sunny but not warm, particularly because of the cool wind which blew off the water. We made our way upstairs to the passenger area from below, where Gramps had parked the van. I stood at the bow of the large vessel and imagined myself an explorer coming to a new land. In many ways, I was.

As the small town of Kingston had come into view, I

spotted what appeared to be a seal bobbing in the water. I pointed and yelled to my grandfather, but my voice got lost in the whoosh of the sea air blowing at us. He nodded his head, though, and smiled.

The boat sounded its horn, signaling for the drivers to return to their cars. Passengers congregated on the top deck, which soon connected with the skybridge on the dock. We walked back down the two flights of stairs, our footsteps echoing on the metal steps, until we reached the van, sandwiched between an RV and an SUV with a tent strapped to the top. We weren't the only ones who'd thought it a good day to begin a camping trip.

When our turn came, we drove off the boat and passed all the cars waiting to take our place on the ferry so they could travel back across the Sound to Edmonds. Seagulls darted about, frantically looking for scraps of whatever they could find that might be edible. There was nothing quite like the sound of seagulls to indicate saltwater nearby.

We drove past some tiny shops and restaurants—a taffy store, a gelato shop, and some sort of greasy spoon burger place—and wove our way through the rest of the town. Soon, we were into a more remote part of the peninsula, with only an occasional gas station, espresso stand, or guy selling chainsaw sculptures in the shapes of eagles and jumping salmon.

The highway curved this way and that, with giant trees covered in lichen and moss lining both sides. Gramps said the forests were filled with Sitka spruce and western hemlock, along with a few yellow cedars.

After a while my eyes grew heavy, and I must have drifted off to sleep because the next sound I'd heard was my grandfather talking to the park ranger. The sign above the ranger's booth read "Salt Creek." I knew we'd arrived because my grandfather had told me the name of the spot where he'd been coming to camp since he was a little boy. He'd taken my mom when she was a little girl as well. I'd heard the stories but had never been there myself.

The other times we'd visited Washington over the years, my mom had said the last thing she wanted to do was sleep outside. My mom was more of a city girl than a country girl, despite having grown up in the area.

The ranger indicated where we were to go, and we headed in that direction. I saw the ocean through my window and some other land beyond in the distance.

"What's that?"

"Canada," my grandfather replied. "This water

is called the Strait of Juan de Fuca. It separates Washington and the United States from Vancouver Island in Canada."

I stared out over the water, which seemed to stretch forever. "I've never seen the border of two countries before. How do they know where in the water the line is?"

"I believe they cut the Strait right down the middle and gave each country half."

"That's pretty cool."

"After your grandmother died, when you were just a baby, I came here a lot. Our old cabin wasn't too far away, but something about being at this spot, well, I felt closer to her here than even in the home we'd shared. We used to come down here with Butch and walk the beach, go crabbing, start a campfire, and boil them right over there." He pointed to an area of the rocky beach, smoother than some of the others. Someone had positioned large pieces of driftwood, which acted like a sectional sofa around a circular pit of stones.

I turned to look at his weathered face, sagging with sadness. "You still miss her a lot."

"Every day. Every single day."

He'd sighed, then, and I found myself feeling the

loss of a woman I didn't remember but really wished I'd known.

Gramps had driven to our designated camping spot for the next two nights and parked the van. When I opened the door, I was immediately hit with the smells of briny saltwater and Christmas tree. Being early July in the Pacific Northwest, the temperature was only about 65 degrees and cloudy. My mother had told me summer weather rarely kicked in before August, one of many reasons she'd gone to sunny Florida.

A breeze blowing off the surface of the ocean gave me a chill, so I zipped my navy-blue hoodie to just below my chin. Gramps went around to the back of the van to begin unloading, and I followed to help. He'd brought a tent, two sleeping bags and pillows, a couple of fishing poles and a tackle box, some firewood, the big white cooler, and the crab pots. I felt certain somewhere in all his stuff was a deck of UNO playing cards and a Yahtzee game box. Knowing my grandfather, he'd also packed chocolate bars, marshmallows, and graham crackers for s'mores. We'd already had s'mores three times around the firepit at his house.

After we unloaded everything from the back of his van, we began to set up the tent. I found the whole thing very confusing, but Gramps had put it together so often we had it up in no time. It wasn't quite lunchtime, so he suggested we walk to the beach.

The dirt path sloped down, and I felt my flip-flops slide a little as I navigated the terrain. I reached the sand at the bottom of the hill, but the sea water had come in and pooled in that area, so my feet got wet. I was pretty impressed with how well Gramps scampered down for an old guy, but I guessed that came with lots of experience.

Quite a bit of driftwood had been strewn around the shore, and I found a perfect walking stick for the hike. The beach was at the center of a cove lined with tall, thick trees. In the middle of the water sat a tiny island, about thirty feet long and about a hundred feet across. The tide was mostly out, so if we'd wanted to, we could have walked all the way out to it. The island reminded me of the kind of place a pirate might bury treasure. It was covered with trees and totally inaccessible except by boat for half the day.

"How long until the tides come in?"

"Oh, I'd say we've got until about dinnertime until this whole area is underwater." Pointing across the sand, his finger traced the horizon as it moved from west to east. "This is called Crescent Bay. Those rocks out there leading to the island are called Tongue Point. It's a protected marine sanctuary, so you can play with the stick, but it has to stay here. Nothing's to be removed, and we must be careful to leave everything as we've found it."

"Do you ever see any animals out here? Like whales?" I hoped to catch a glimpse of something I could brag about when I got back to Florida in late August for school.

"Oh, sure. I've seen lots of harbor seals and otters, and every once in a while, an orca or a gray whale. Of course, you'll also see deer hiking these paths and eagles flying overhead." He stopped walking and stared in the direction of the far point of the crescent, a spot dense with trees. "Sometimes you might even encounter something else."

I'd never seen my grandfather look so odd. "Something else...like what?"

Based on his expression, I wasn't quite sure I wanted to know the answer.

He looked back to me and shook his head. "Never mind. Five dollars if you spot a bald eagle before me."

"No fair!" I complained. "You've got the eagle eye."

"But Jake," he'd said. "You're my grandson, which means you've inherited the eagle eye as well. It's a skill which comes in mighty handy around these parts. You always need to keep your eyes open."

6

A Squad Is Born

The day after my meeting with Jasmine at the park, I approached her by her locker.

"Here." I shoved my homemade business card at her.

Startled, she grabbed the piece of paper I'd carefully cut just to size, looked it over, and laughed. "What am I supposed to do with this?" She waved the flimsy paper. "There's not even a phone number." Her glossy pink lips pursed into a smirk.

Sheepishly I responded, "Yeah, I don't have one. I'm thinking about setting up an email, though. I can't use my school email for the business." I shrugged my shoulders. "It's a start, at least. Besides, you already know where to find me."

"So, you're gonna take my case?"

"I am."

"Cool. Did you figure out how much to charge me for your services? I have some allowance, but it needs to be reasonable. I'm saving up to get a really good pair of headphones."

"Well, you're in luck, then. I thought maybe I could do this one job pro bono, and then if you hear of anyone else who needs my specific type of skills, you could send them my way. I'd give you a referral bonus."

I'd thought a lot about the idea the night before. If I charged Jasmine five or ten dollars, once the case had been resolved one way or another, she'd probably go back to never talking to me again. I'd end up exactly where I'd started. However, if I did it for free but with some strings attached, there was a chance I could actually break into the social scene of Hawthorne's sixth-grade class. I wasn't desperate, but we were a month into the school year and so far, I'd only made one friend, Lanny, who was really more like a mascot.

I'd also made an enemy, Michael, who had a mascot

of his own. Charlie parroted anything Michael said.

Jasmine scrunched her nose in confusion, her tiny brown freckles getting pushed into each other. "What is…pro bono, and what do you mean by referral bonus?"

"Pro bono means I do it for free, sorta. Instead of you paying me with money, you pay me by helping me get more clients. Let's say I charge them five or ten dollars for their case, then I'd give you a buck or two for sending them my way. It's a symbiotic relationship." I finished my explanation with my best attempt at a convincing smile.

"Simbi- what?" She shook her head. "You sure use a lot of big words, Jake. I'm surprised you're not in highly capable."

"I could've been, but I didn't want to do it. Symbiotic means it works for both of us. We work together, so we both benefit. It's what they like to call a mutually beneficial situation. A win-win. You in?"

She tilted her head in thought for a minute. "A win-win. I suppose that might be a good thing." She slowly nodded her head. "You're right. I could be your partner."

"Now wait a minute, that's not what I said," I protested. "I work alone."

Jasmine's hands went straight to her hips in defiance.

"Look, if we're gonna have a...simba...simbaotic relationship, or whatever you called it, a win-win, we need to come to an agreement we can both live with. I have connections, so you need me. You have the expertise. If we work together as a team, as partners, we'll be way more successful than if you try to do this all on your own."

Out of nowhere, Lanny appeared next to her. "Partners! I'm in!"

I rolled my eyes. "Now look what you've done. Don't I get any say in what happens in my company?"

"Look, you can try to go it alone if that's really what you want." She bobbed her head back and forth with attitude. "Have it your way, but I'd rather pay the five dollars than have you take advantage of my popularity while I get nothing in return. I'm the one taking the risks. It's my reputation on the line. You'd be passing up a once-in-a-lifetime opportunity to work with me, and that doesn't sound like good business."

I looked between the two of them and sighed. "Fine, we can be a team, but not partners. I'm the president, Jasmine is the vice president—"

"Co-president," she interrupted.

"Vice president," I repeated. "And Lanny, you

can be..." I stopped to think. "You can be executive assistant."

I didn't really know what an executive assistant did, but it was the job title my mom had held back in Florida, and it was all I could come up with in the spur of the moment. Lanny beamed with pride, and I wondered if he knew what it meant, either.

Jasmine looked at the card in her hand. "This isn't your only one, is it?"

I shrugged my shoulders with embarrassment.

"You made one business card. Okay, well, we're gonna need to make some more of these, for each of us with our names and titles, and on better paper, too. I have a cell phone, so I can put my number on there, but Jake, you should get an email like you talked about. You can get one for free. My mom can order the cards once we have all the information."

"She'd really do that?"

"Of course. She does whatever I want." Jasmine flipped her hair over her shoulder.

I didn't know what to say because my mom definitely didn't do whatever I wanted...not that I asked much of her. It wasn't that she was mean or anything. She wasn't around much because she drove to work in traffic every day, worked long hours, and then drove home in traffic. Even though she had a good job, we didn't have a lot of extra money because she was saving up for us to buy a house of our own. She always said Seattle real estate was "bonkers" compared to Orlando. I figured that meant expensive. That's why I felt bad asking for anything, especially a cell phone, even though I was pretty sure I was the only sixth grader in America who didn't have one...maybe even the whole world. If I wasn't, it sure felt that way.

When Michael's phone had broken, I'd sat in the office with a stomachache, thinking how upset my mom was going to be. Thankfully, Mrs. Farnsworth, the principal, had concluded it was an accident. When she'd called Michael's dad, the sheriff, to tell him what had happened, he'd told her they'd purchased insurance for the phone, and it would be easily replaced. They'd never even needed to call my mom or grandfather. No harm, no foul...unless you counted me gaining a nemesis for life.

"Cool, well, I'd better get to class. I guess we should set up a meeting. Lanny, Jasmine and I have second lunch. What lunch do you have?"

"Hi-caps have second lunch with the fifth and sixth

graders." He wore a smug expression.

"Really? I wonder why I've never seen you."

"I'm usually helping Mr. Tucker in the library."

"Of course, you are. Okay, everybody, let's meet by the swings at lunch recess. We can formulate our strategy then."

Jasmine nodded her head and shut her locker. "Sounds good."

Lanny put his hand out, and Jasmine and I both looked at him in confusion.

"What are you doing?" she asked.

"I thought we'd make it official with some sort of hands in/hands out kind of thing. You know, like when the basketball team finishes their talk during time-out." His eyes were hopeful and so wide open the tips of his long lashes nearly touched his eyebrows, which were arched with excitement.

Jasmine and I looked at each other, shrugged our shoulders, glanced around to make sure no one was watching, and put our hands into the middle of the circle before quickly lifting them out. We were officially a squad.

• • •

At the first lunch recess meeting of Sasquatch Hunters of Washington, Inc., we formalized our company structure. I, Jake Q. Nelson, was declared President and CEO, Jasmine Davis became vice president, and Laniban "Lanny" Mahajan was named executive assistant. We decided Lanny's job was to keep all our records. He already had a notebook and pencil at the ready to take notes. Jasmine was to be in charge of marketing and also, apparently, being generally bossy without actually being the boss. My job was to oversee the investigations.

Since we already had our first case—Jasmine's—we created a list with our next steps.

1) A night investigation was in order. Being October in Washington, the sun usually set by about 6:30 pm, so we could conceivably do it Friday night around 7:30 or 8 and still be home at a reasonable time.

2) Prior to that, I needed to conduct interviews with Danielle Arroyo, Kayla Kim, and Erika Herschel. Jasmine was embarrassed to talk to her friends, but I had a feeling one of them may have seen more than she thought. Jasmine promised to set up the interviews by

telling them she was helping me with a research project and needed their input.

3) Jasmine would create and order the business cards, with her mother's help, of course.

"What am I s'posed to do?" Lanny asked.

"You can come along and keep track of everything that's said and everything that happens. We're gonna need proof of our methods and sources if we want to be taken seriously with our discoveries."

His tiny chest puffed with my description of the importance of his role.

"We should make a pact to not reveal anything to anyone outside of this group," Jasmine insisted. "Everything must remain confidential until or unless we are all in agreement."

"I concur."

Both of them looked at me with their eyebrows scrunched together.

"That means I agree."

They nodded their heads.

"Discretion, which means keeping information to yourself, is going to be really important. We don't want anyone messing up our plans, especially Michael and Charlie. And we definitely don't want to tell anyone anything which might get us in trouble. Deal?"

"Deal!" they answered in unison.

Out of the corner of my eye, I caught Michael watching us. I couldn't tell what he was thinking, but he was definitely paying attention to us. We were going to have to be more careful about meeting in public. I wouldn't put it past Michael to squash Sasquatch Hunters before we'd even solved our first case.

The Interviews

Before I got on the bus to go home that afternoon, Jasmine pulled me aside to hand me a piece of paper with her friends' phone numbers on it.

"These are Danielle and Kayla's cell numbers. Erika has a cell phone, but her parents only let her use it to call family, so she may not answer. Leave a message, and she'll call you back from her home phone. Erika is the one who wouldn't go into the woods after watching Danielle and Kayla go back. Kayla is super funny. Danielle can be…well, she's bossy."

I was thinking, *it takes one to know one*, but said

nothing, hoping my face didn't show what was on my mind.

When I got on the bus, Lanny waved at me to sit next to him.

"What did Jasmine want? I need to know if it's something I should write in my notebook. I have to be kept in the loop on everything."

"She gave me this list of her friends' names and phone numbers." I waved it in front of him. "Kayla Kim, Danielle Arroyo, and Erika Herschel."

"Wow." Lanny breathed with awe. "That's a valuable piece of paper."

I nodded solemnly. "I know."

We both stared at the paper as if it were a sacred relic.

"Who do you think I should talk to first?"

"I'd go with Kayla. She's friends with my sister Tanvi, even though Tanvi is in seventh grade. They play on the same soccer team. She's come over to our house a lot, and she's very nice. I'd save Danielle for last because she scares me." Lanny gave an involuntary shudder.

"I got the impression from Jasmine that Danielle's kind of intense, so I think that's a good plan. I just need to ask questions which won't give away our investigation or embarrass Jasmine. She'll never forgive me if her friends start making fun of her." I hadn't yet figured out how to get them to talk about that night in the woods without also revealing what Jasmine had seen or betraying her trust.

• • •

When I walked through the front door to my grandfather's house, he was nowhere to be seen. The bandsaw was whining in the back shop, so I went to see what he was doing. On his workbench was a wooden rocking horse. Gramps was cutting half of an oblong piece which would fit around the horse's neck as a collar when connected to the other half. He turned off the saw and looked over at me standing in the doorway.

"You comin' in, or you just gonna stand there like a statue?" He wiped dust off the wood's surface with a rag.

I stepped into the shop and approached the rocking horse.

"Who's this for?" I ran my fingertips over the curves of the animal. It had been sanded but had yet to be varnished and polished.

"Margot's granddaughter Lily."

Margot was his next-door neighbor.

"Lily's turning three, and she loves horses. Margot had seen the one I'd made for your mother years ago and asked if I could make one for Lily. She offered to pay me an obscene amount of money, which I refused, of course." He grabbed the two crescent-shaped pieces, wood glue, and a vise to hold them together while the glue set.

"What do you mean, of course? Why wouldn't you take her money?"

He set the objects in his hands on the table and turned to look at me. "What I do in here is a labor of love. It's the outward expression of my passions, my dreams. Charging money would cheapen it. Besides," he added. "I like Margot."

And then he did something I'd never before seen him do. He winked.

"You *like* her-like her?" I was incredulous. "Like, you wanna take her on a date?"

I couldn't imagine Gramps on a date, with his salt-and-pepper chin-length hair slicked back and a bouquet of flowers in his nervous, clammy hands.

"Hey now, I'm old, but I'm not dead. Your

grandmother's been gone a very long time, and a little company's sounding pretty good. I want someone to share my life with. I thought that would be Valerie, but fate intervened." He took the collar pieces, glued each end of one piece, and held them together. "Do you think you could put the vise on for me? You just need to open it a bit by cranking the shaft."

I picked up the blue metal vise and turned the crank like I was playing with a jack-in-the-box until the opening was wide enough to slide over the plywood.

"Okay, now position the vise over the wood here where I'm holding it and then crank it tight again."

I did as he asked, rotating the handle until it resisted going any tighter.

"Perfect!" He crowed, and I felt myself swell with pride.

We both stood back and admired the horse.

"What comes next? After the collar dries, I mean."

"Well, I've got some more sanding to do, to make sure it's totally smooth, and then I'll do a few coats of polyurethane. That'll give it a nice gloss. I'll attach the mane and tail hair and some facial features. What do you think for the eyes, blue, brown, or green?"

After a moment of staring at the horse, I asked, "What color are Lily's eyes?"

Gramps smiled. "I like the way you think. She's got black curly hair and brown eyes, so we'll give her a horse who has the same."

I dug my toe into the dusty ground of the workshop, nervous to ask my question. "Gramps, do you mind if I make a few phone calls?"

Tilting his head, he appraised me silently. "Of course, Jake. This is your home too now, for the time being at least. Everything okay?"

"Yeah, I just need to do some interviews for...a project. I have three people I need to talk to."

I specifically avoided telling him they were all girls and what project I was working on. I hoped he'd believe it was for a school report or presentation. I wasn't ready to have another conversation about it, especially since the last time we'd talked about it, he'd made it clear he didn't like the idea of me pursuing squatch hunting if it meant potentially making him the laughingstock of Hawthorne.

He didn't ask for more details, and I didn't volunteer them. He went back to working on the rocking horse, humming a happy tune. It felt good to see him happy.

I walked into the kitchen and poured myself a big glass of pink lemonade. Pulling the piece of paper Jasmine had given me out of my pocket, I took a deep breath and picked up the phone from its cradle on the counter. I had a feeling I'd be less intimidated talking to an actual Sasquatch than to these girls. At the sound of the dial tone, I slowly pressed each number until I heard ringing on the other end of the line.

"Hello?" The voice came on after a click.

"Hi, is this Kayla?" I tapped my pencil's eraser nervously on the notepad I'd set in front of me in case she said anything I'd want to relay to Jasmine and Lanny.

"Hi, Jake."

I was startled by her forthrightness.

"How'd you know it was me?"

"Jasmine told me you'd be calling. She didn't tell me what it was about, though." Kayla's voice had a sparkle to it, the kind of voice generally happy people tended to have, so it calmed my nerves.

"Jasmine's helping me work on a project, and I was hoping maybe you would be willing to help me too." I was trying to be careful not to tip her off to the extent of Jasmine's involvement. Once again, I tapped my eraser against the notepad.

"I guess it depends on what you want me to do." She sounded wary.

"I want to ask you a few questions. Anything you say will be kept confidential." Tap-tap.

"Questions about what?" She was getting exasperated, which didn't bode well for her cooperation.

"The night you and Jasmine and Erika and Danielle snuck out to go to the woods."

A sharp intake of air came from the other end of the line, and I knew I had her full attention.

"Don't worry, Kayla, I'm not going to tell anyone what you say to me. There are just some things I'm trying to figure out, and Jasmine said you would be a good person to talk to. I've never been there in the dark, only in the daytime, and I didn't go all the way back, but I've heard rumors about various things people have seen, and I am trying to find out if any of them are real." I hoped by leaving my agenda vague and not mentioning that Jasmine had hired me, I'd be protecting her privacy.

"She…she told you about that?" Kayla's voice quieted

and deepened. Gone was the perky happy tone, replaced by one much more serious.

"She did. I know you only stayed in there for less than a minute, but did you see or hear anything unusual?" I was doing my best to not freak her out, but it seemed I was failing miserably.

A sigh blew through the phone. "Unusual?"

"Anything…unexpected, out of the ordinary." I held my breath in anticipation of her response.

She cleared her throat. She was struggling with something, but what it was I couldn't say. Perhaps she was worried about getting in trouble. Maybe she saw what Jasmine saw and didn't want to get teased. It made sense since it was what Jasmine feared. It could also be she was embarrassed about being in there for the shortest amount of time other than Erika, who'd never even ventured into the woods.

"By the way, what was the bet about, anyway? I tried to pry it out of Jasmine, but she wouldn't tell me."

Almost immediately, I realized this question was a mistake. Not only did it change the subject just as she was on the verge of telling me about her experience, but it also caused her to shut down completely.

"Why would you think I'd tell you, a total stranger, what Jasmine wouldn't? Is that what this is? You're just trying to get me to give up secrets because Jasmine won't? Sorry, dude. Not happening!" She growled in frustration and ended the call.

This was really bad. Not only had I managed to get on the wrong side of the nicest of the three girls I needed to talk to, but I'd also done it before getting even a tiny bit of information out of her. I should have known better than to push the issue of the bet. Jasmine had also been weird about it, so my curiosity had gotten the best of me, and it had backfired. Big time.

I stared at the list of phone numbers, rolled my shoulders back, stretched my neck first to one side, then the other, and picked up the phone again. This time I was determined to stay away from the subject of the bet.

"Hi, this is Erika. I can't come to the phone right now. Leave a message, and I'll call you back."

I had to admit to myself I was relieved to get her voicemail.

"Uh, hi, Erika. This is Jake Nelson, from school. Jasmine gave me your number. Hopefully she told you I'd be calling. Call me back when you get a chance." I gave my grandfather's home number and hung up.

I was down to one number, and I dreaded making the call. I'd had very little experience with Danielle in the month since school started. All I knew about her was that when my teacher Mr. Stevens asked a question, Danielle's hand was the first to be raised. Also, Lanny was scared of her. Lanny was skittish as a general rule, though.

I reached for the phone, but before I had the chance to pick it up, it rang.

"H-hello? I, uh, I mean, Nelson residence. Jake speaking."

My grandfather had insisted I improve my phone manners. Back in Florida, the only calls I got were from my mom and people trying to sell something.

"It's Danielle Arroyo. I heard you wanted to talk to me."

I almost dropped the phone onto the kitchen floor. "D-Danielle! How did you know I was just about to call you?"

"Well first, Jasmine told me. Then Kayla called. She's super mad at you right now. She wanted to warn me you're snooping. Are you sticking your nose where it doesn't belong?"

Although her words were harsh, I was surprised to

realize I wasn't all that scared of her. She had a high-pitched voice like Minnie Mouse, so her tough-girl routine was hard to take too seriously.

"Jasmine's helping me solve the mystery of the woods by the school. I know you girls were out there the other night, and I wanna know what happened."

Even though I didn't have the right to know, I figured Danielle was the kind of girl who'd appreciate a direct approach. I was right.

"I stayed back there the longest," she preened. "Did Jasmine tell you that?"

"She did. She said you were the bravest out of everyone." I'd heard a little flattery went a long way, especially with know-it-alls. "Did you see anything out of the ordinary when you were back there?"

"It was pretty dark. I've been back there during the day before, so I knew the area. There's a giant tree, and even though I've never seen anyone, it looks like people have been there. It's probably just high schoolers trying to vape or drink alcohol. They're stupid like that," she scoffed.

"So, for five whole minutes you were back there, and you saw nothing?"

"Not really. I thought I heard something in the bushes, and it smelled funky like sour apple candy mixed with crusty gym socks, but when I looked, it was just blackness."

"You weren't scared?" I tapped my eraser several times, imagining the scene and how I might have felt.

"Sure, I was, but I did what my dad taught me. He's a lawyer, you know. Anyway, he always says, 'Mija, when you are afraid just remember you are strong and brave. Don't let fear keep you from doing whatever you want to do.' I just kept repeating over and over, 'I'm strong and brave and not afraid. I'm strong and brave and not afraid.'"

As she said it, I believed her. I also thought her dad might be onto something.

"And it worked?" I stopped tapping.

"I won, didn't I? There was no way I was letting fear be the reason I didn't get—" she stopped abruptly. "I mean, I wasn't gonna let fear keep me from being the best. I'm always the best, and it's gonna stay that way."

I really wanted to ask her what she was going to say before she stopped herself, but after what had happened with Kayla, I couldn't take that chance. "Anything else I should know?"

"Hmmm," she sang in a melodic arc of descending notes like a slide whistle. "I can't think of anything right now, but if I do, I'll call you back. Or I can text you."

My neck warmed with shame and embarrassment. "I don't have a cell phone. I was just about to make an email account. When I get it done, I'll give it to you, and you can send me messages that way."

"Weird. Okay, well, I gotta go. Horseback riding lessons. See you tomorrow."

She hung up, and I slumped into the chair at the breakfast table. I'd survived my encounter with Danielle in one piece. Barely.

8

Close Encounters of The Squatch Kind

That night as I laid in bed unable to sleep, I wrestled with telling my grandfather about Sasquatch Hunters. I wasn't sure what was holding me back. Sure, he had his reasons for not wanting to talk about his own encounter, but it didn't mean he wouldn't be a good resource, and it didn't mean he wouldn't support what I was trying to accomplish. Also, he was the first man in my life I'd ever felt I could trust.

Truthfully, he was the only man in my life. Mom didn't date much, and when she did, she made sure never to bring any of them around. Good thing, too, since none of those relationships had lasted. I'd asked her once if she thought she'd ever find a husband. She'd just sighed and said, "From your lips to God's ears." I was ten at the time, so I didn't really know what she meant. I figured it had something to do with answered prayers...or unanswered prayers, in her case.

The night Gramps had told me his story, the one which got me interested in all this Sasquatch stuff in the first place, I couldn't sleep either. After setting up our campsite, we'd spent the day exploring Crescent Bay and Salt Creek.

The park was nearly two hundred acres and included the abandoned bunkers of Camp Hayden. During World War II, the area was called Striped Peak Military Reservation, and it was created initially to protect the entrance to Puget Sound. It was renamed Camp Hayden for Brigadier General John L. Hayden, who'd commanded the Puget Sound Harbor Defenses. The camp had been abandoned by the Army in 1948. As many as one hundred and fifty soldiers were stationed there at the height of the war. What was left were the remnants of two concrete bunkers which had once housed sixteen-inch cannons. There were also still a few other smaller bunkers.

I'd pretended to be an important Naval commander

giving orders to fire on the invaders, and Gramps had humored me by responding, "Aye-aye, Captain!" It was a fun day, and I only thought about missing my mom once.

That night the flames of our campfire had licked the cool ocean breeze which blew in from the strait. The fire had crackled and sparked, embers dancing in the air before my mesmerized eyes. A small stream of smoke slithered into the sky where wisps of clouds were pulled across a palette of stars. I had a belly full of hot dogs and marshmallows. The combination of fresh air, an active day, and the lull of the warm blaze had caused my eyelids to droop.

I was wrapped in a white wool blanket with red, green, blue, and yellow stripes. Gramps had leaned back against a large log, his boots crossed in front of him and his hands clasped behind his neck. He was quiet for the longest time, and when he spoke, it was in his typical calm, hushed way. This time, though, there was a reticence I'd never heard in his voice before. He seemed uncertain. I couldn't remember another incident in all our interactions where he'd given me the impression of uncertainty.

"The people of this land, the Elwha Klallam, sometimes spoke of a being called čičayíkʷtən."

"Chick kay ick twin?"

"Close." He chuckled. "You've probably heard him referred to by other names such as Sasquatch or Bigfoot."

My tired eyes had flown open, no longer drifting off to sleep. I opened my mouth to question him, but he'd also opened his mouth to begin speaking again, so I waited for him to continue.

"I spent the bulk of my childhood about twenty miles away from where we sit tonight. Growing up around here, I'd never really believed in the stories of the wild man, even the one about Boston Charlie's encounter at Cat Peak."

"Boston Charlie?" I sat up and pulled the wool blanket tight around me to keep the chill out. Whether the chill was coming from without or within, I couldn't say.

"Boston Charlie's Camp near Mount Carrie is named for a Klallam man who used to hunt elk in the Olympic Mountains. He lived to be about one hundred years old. The story goes that one day he was out hunting and got injured. For days he lay there, unable to help himself. One evening, just as the sun was setting, a large being appeared. Charlie was certain he was about to be killed by the creature, but instead it had placed dew-covered berries in his mouth. Because of the kindness of the giant, Charlie survived until he was rescued."

Just then, one of the red-hot logs in the firepit had snapped and broken in half. Ashes plumed like an eruption.

"That's it?" I was disappointed. "That's the end of the story? A Bigfoot came and gave him wet fruit and then left and that's it?"

I felt robbed of a more exciting ending to what sounded like just another old legend. He'd already told me a few of them that summer as we'd sat in front of the living room fireplace or outside around the firepit. This one was by far the least satisfying.

"That's the thing about real Bigfoot encounters, as opposed to fabricated ones. Outside of the fact you're looking at the face of a giant hairy man who's not supposed to exist, the experiences tend to be pretty mundane." He stoked the fire with a long stick.

I watched his face as light and shadows moved across it, and tried to read his expression to see if he was joking. There wasn't even a glimmer of a smirk or a smile. In fact, he'd appeared deadly serious.

"W-what do you mean by real Bigfoot encounters?" The tingling sensation of fear moved up my neck as if a bug were crawling along my vertebrae. I swatted at it just to make sure there wasn't one.

"I've seen those crazy TV shows, and they're nothing like what happened to me." He paused and looked at me. My face probably showed the shock I felt, because he said, "I don't mean to scare you, boy. It's just being out here…well, it reminds me of that night. I had come out here not long after your grandmother passed. It was January, so the campground was empty. The sun set by five o'clock, before I'd even had a chance to cook myself some chili for supper. I was planning on sleeping in the van, as the temperature was supposed to get down to near-freezing, but I had a good blaze going and there was no way I was eatin' cold chili from a tin can." He picked up a piece of driftwood and tossed it in the campfire. "Anyway, I was sitting here, nothing but the sound of the wind through the pines, the water lapping the rocks on the shore, the crackling of the fire, and an occasional hoot or howl to keep me company. Or so I thought…"

My chest thumped, and my breathing quickened and became shallow. I was on the verge of hyperventilating like the time at summer camp in Orlando when we'd run an obstacle course in 95 degrees and 100% humidity.

"Were you scared?" I whispered, irrationally fearful

any sound I made might actually summon the creature.

"I think I was too stunned to be scared at first."

"How did you know it wasn't an owl or a deer?"

"At first I smelled him. It was like fish and rotting cabbage and my nostrils stung with the stench. I figured someone had hit a skunk out on the highway, causing the odor to waft into the park. I've experienced the smell before and it can be pretty pungent. It was when I heard the breathing, a rumbly sound like my uncle's phlegmy lungs just before he died of emphysema, only louder and more full-bodied."

I'd wanted to ask what emphysema was, but I didn't want to interrupt the story, so I made a mental note to myself to Google it later.

"He was at the edge of the campground where it meets the forest, and his eyes glowed like a cat's. I'd say he was about seven and a half feet tall, and he just stood there, not doing anything but watching me."

"What did you do? Did you pee your pants? I totally would have peed my pants." I was babbling from nervous excitement. I couldn't believe what I was hearing, and yet I wanted to believe it with all my heart and soul. If my grandfather was making up this story, I was going to feel like the biggest fool in the world.

"You're not making this up to spook me, are you? Are you just messing with me?"

Instead of getting defensive, Gramps had slowly shaken his head. "I wish I were making it up. And no, I didn't pee my britches, but I froze. Not my finest moment. They say when faced with extreme danger, the human body has one of three responses, fight, flight, or freeze. I think it would have been a mistake to try and fight a giant beast, even though he wasn't acting aggressive, and I didn't have my shotgun with me. I could have run to my van, but my feet felt as if they were cement cinder blocks. I guess if he'd have moved toward me, my flight instinct might have kicked in, but he didn't. He just stood there watching me for a few seconds, although it felt like hours, and then he turned and left. It was as if he was simply curious about the noise since the park's usually vacant during January, and when he saw me decided I wasn't a threat."

"What did you do after he left?" I was sitting on my hands to keep from chewing my fingernails. It was a bad habit I had when I was nervous.

"It took a bit before I realized I'd been holding my breath. I sat there in a stupor trying to determine whether I'd been asleep and just didn't know it. I slapped my cheeks a couple times, but sure enough, I was wide awake. I watched the forest's edge for about twenty minutes waiting for him to return, but he never did. I doused my fire, hopped in the van, and drove to Port Angeles to get a motel room. I kept replaying it over and over in my head, trying to rationalize what I'd seen...but I couldn't." He'd stared at the fire as if it held the answers, and then, after a few moments, slapped his hands on his thighs once he decided it didn't. "We'd better get you to bed. Big day crabbing tomorrow!" He stood and wiped the dirt off his Levi's, as if he hadn't just told me a life-changing, mind-blowing story.

I'd wanted to ask more questions, but I could tell the subject was closed as far as Gramps was concerned. I didn't know how he expected me to be able to sleep after hearing his story. I'd laid in our tent listening for any noises that sounded like an animal, but it was difficult to hear anything over the sound of Gramps snoring.

My grandfather had told me what should have been an unbelievable story, if it weren't for the fact that he was a man I believed completely, that is. He'd never lied to me before, and although he had a good sense of humor, he wasn't one for pranks.

After that trip, I'd gone home to Orlando and done as much research on Bigfoot sightings as I could. It had opened a whole new world to me. I spent all my free time learning about the different creatures that fell under the category of cryptid. I'd never heard the term before, but suddenly it was my new favorite word. The Oxford English Dictionary defined a cryptid as an animal whose existence or survival to the present day was disputed or unsubstantiated.

Scientists have said we live on a big, mostly unknown planet. The heart of jungles, the most remote parts of the forests, and the deepest parts of the ocean have remained largely unexplored, and every year, 15,000 new species of plants and animals are discovered. Several species have been thought to have gone extinct, only to be found very much alive. Before they were discovered and documented, the platypus, the giant squid, and the Komodo dragon were all considered cryptids.

When Captain John Hunter sent a platypus pelt back to England in 1789, it was dismissed as a hoax. After two years and other eyewitnesses testifying to the existence of the animal, scientists finally accepted the duck-billed, beaver-tailed, egg-laying mammal as real. His story convinced me that just because people believed something didn't exist, it didn't mean they were right.

If my grandfather said he saw Bigfoot, I believed he saw Bigfoot. Now I just had to set about proving it.

Sightings in the southeastern United States were much different than those in the Pacific Northwest, I'd found. In Florida we had what was referred to as a "skunk ape," and it was located mostly in Dade County, near Miami. I lived in Orlando, which was about a three to four-hour drive north on the I-95 interstate. I came across a story which said a Bigfoot was spotted running into the Apalachicola National Forest outside of Tallahassee on the panhandle a few years back, but that was at least a four-hour drive from my house as well. My neck of the woods, so to speak, had no actual woods to explore, which made a sighting pretty much impossible.

My new home state of Washington, though, was nothing but trees. When we'd arrived in August right before school started, I'd made my mom drive the Mountain Loop Highway, where many sightings had been reported over several decades. In the 1970's, near the town of Granite Falls alone, there were seven reports. Unfortunately, we saw nothing but a few deer.

Near Gramps' neighborhood there'd been recent sightings of coyotes and bears roaming the vicinity, and most Sasquatch researchers believed where there were deer and coyotes and bears, there were also squatches. I'd heard Bigfoots liked to hide their howls among the howls of coyotes so as to not be detected. They were smart like that.

In bed in my new house, well, Gramps' house, in my new town, a year and a half after hearing about his encounter while sitting by the campfire at Salt Creek, I had the same buzzing excitement I'd felt the night my world view had changed forever. After hearing Jasmine's story, I thought there was a real possibility Hawthorne's woods might actually be home to the mythical beast. I'd finally made some new friends and they wanted to be partners in my endeavors. Also, Jasmine had helped me see that if we were able to prove the existence of the legendary Bigfoot, I too would become legendary. My picture would be in newspapers around the world, on CNN, and all over the internet. The only way my dad wouldn't hear about me was if he lived off the grid somewhere…or if he was dead. I didn't want to think about that possibility, though.

After getting off on the wrong foot with Michael on my very first day of school, I'd dreaded the rest of the year, thinking I'd already blown any chance I had of fitting in, but Jasmine was popular—and pretty—and she wanted to be part of this adventure with me. Lanny, well, he was kind of annoying, but he was smart and funny, and our little trio had made me feel at home for the first time since I'd arrived.

As I finally drifted off to sleep, I imagined images of the three of us becoming internet famous all over TikTok, Twitter, YouTube, and the news as they talked about our brilliant, historic discovery. Then I pictured a "big man in more ways than one"—aka my father—sitting on his couch in Florida watching TV. When he saw my name and face, he jumped up and yelled, "that's my boy!"

I must have already fallen asleep by that point in my fantasy, though, because when the man's face was finally visible, it was covered in hair. In my dream, my dad was a Bigfoot.

It Happened One Night Investigation

Friday was the big night investigation, and Jasmine had invited Lanny and me to come over for dinner. It gave us something to tell our parents so they wouldn't be wondering why we were wandering around in the woods in the dark with no supervision, if they'd even allow it in the first place. I didn't think my mom would be thrilled with that plan.

When I left the house, Gramps mentioned he was concerned my dark clothing made me hard to see as I rode my bike to Jasmine's. What he didn't know was I'd purposely worn those clothes to be incognito so I wouldn't be seen sneaking into the woods. I insisted I would be fine, reminding him my helmet had a reflective stripe, as did my spokes, and I had green LED lights around the tires. He made me promise I would call him if I needed a ride home because it had gotten too dark.

My mom pulled into the driveway from work as I was leaving. She stopped to roll down her window. "Hey. You're off to Jasmine's?"

"Yep." I didn't want to prolong the conversation. I was anxious to get to Jasmine's house to have dinner and make our plan. I also didn't want my mom asking too many questions.

"You've got your backpack with you. Will you be doing homework?"

"Dunno. Maybe." I shrugged.

"Did you have a good day?"

I groaned inwardly but just nodded my head.

She sighed the sigh of exasperated mothers everywhere. "Fine, you can go, but tomorrow morning I'm making Dutch babies, so don't stay out too late. I don't want you sleeping in, so I think you should be home by 9:30 tonight."

"Ugh, okay."

"I love you," she said as I rode away.

"I love you too," I called out, not looking back but waving my hand over my head in a goodbye.

At least I'd get Dutch babies, even if I didn't get to sleep in. Dutch babies were puffy pancakes baked in a casserole dish or skillet. Made with lots of butter, my mom always served them sprinkled with powdered sugar and drenched in syrup. It was definitely worth getting up before the crack of noon on a Saturday morning to eat them hot and fresh.

When I arrived at Jasmine's neighborhood, I couldn't believe how big the houses were. There was a huge gate at the entrance to the private cul-de-sac of mansions on the golf course. There was a box for calling the residents to let you inside the neighborhood. There were only eight names listed, so I easily found the button next to "Davis" and pressed it. There was a beep, followed by another one, and then Jasmine's voice came through the speaker.

"Hello?"

"Hi Jasmine, it's Jake. I'm at the gate."

"I know, silly." She laughed. "There's a camera in the

call-box. I'm looking right at you."

I looked closely at the box and saw a tiny circle where the camera must have been and waved. One long beep sounded, and the gate began to swing open.

"Once you get through the gate, turn to the left. We're the gray house with black shutters. Lanny's already here. His parents dropped him off about ten minutes ago."

Once the gate had opened wide enough, I rode my bike through and turned left. Jasmine's house wasn't difficult to find, as it was straight ahead at the end of the cul-de-sac and was exactly as she described. It was also enormous. The driveway was longer than the length of the parking lot at our apartment complex in Orlando.

Jasmine was standing in the doorway. The light shining from behind her caused her hair to glow more golden than normal. She, like me, was also wearing dark clothes, so although her face looked like an angel, she wasn't dressed like one. She looked like a really pretty cat burglar.

Lanny popped up beside her. "Did you get the night scope?" He yelled this, as if we weren't trying to be super secretive.

Both Jasmine and I shushed him at the same time.

"We don't need the whole neighborhood to know what we're doing. Yes, I got the night scope."

"Sorry, I'm just so excited!" His face was beaming, and truthfully, his enthusiasm was contagious.

Earlier that day, we'd met by the swings at lunch recess to discuss what items we'd need to properly conduct the night investigation. I'd offered to "borrow" my grandfather's infrared scope he used for hunting. What I meant was I planned to take it without his permission and put it back before he even knew it was gone. After school, I'd snuck into the garage, stuffed the scope down my sock, and covered it with my pant leg. When I'd gotten to my room with my stash, I'd shoved it into the bottom of my backpack.

Lanny was in charge of bringing his journal and a flashlight.

Jasmine had said she'd pop some popcorn—because everyone knew Bigfoots liked popcorn—and she'd also bring a pair of castanets she'd gotten on her spring break trip to Puerto Vallarta.

"What are castanets?" Lanny had asked.

"They're a musical instrument with two round pieces

of wood connected on one side by a rubber band. When you open and close them with your finger and thumb like this," Jasmine mimicked the movement, "they make a click-clacking sound."

"It's a good idea." I nodded. "Anything living in the woods will be drawn to unusual smells and noises."

"You mean any Bigfoots living in the woods." Lanny gave an involuntary shudder.

"Hey, if this is too scary for you, Lanny, you don't have to go. Jasmine and I can handle it on our own."

Lanny had jutted his chin. "I'm not scared."

He was scared. We all were, but our curiosity was stronger than our fear...at least in the middle of the day on our school playground. Now that the sun was starting to go down, it was a different story.

"You guys ready for this adventure?" I pulled out my kickstand and leaned my bike against it.

They both nodded their heads, but neither of them was very convincing.

I followed Jasmine into her house, with Lanny right behind me. I tried to play it cool, even though it was the fanciest and biggest house I'd ever set foot inside. In the entry was a large staircase with super tall ceilings and railing surrounding the upper hallway. To my left was a dining room enclosed by glass doors and to the right was an office. Above me was a huge crystal chandelier which had so many bulbs it must have taken someone an hour to change them all.

Jasmine led us through a look-but-don't-touch kind of living room where no one ever hung out and into a giant kitchen. Six benches were tucked beneath the center island. In the corner, right next to the refrigerator, a spiral staircase led upstairs. I'd never seen a couch and TV in a kitchen before.

A woman with hair similar to Jasmine's but darker stood over the stove, stirring whatever was in the skillet with a giant wooden spoon. She smiled at us as we came in the room. "You must be Jake." She waved the spoon. "I'd come shake your hand, but I'm a little occupied right now. Do you like beef tacos? I also have beans in case you don't eat meat like Lanny."

"Yes, ma'am, thank you. Tacos are one of my favorite foods."

My mom had taught me to be polite when at other people's houses for dinner, but she also never forced me to lie to spare their feelings. Good thing tacos really were one of my favorite things to eat. I was grateful she wasn't making something gourmet, since the house was so fancy. I'd heard some fancy people like to eat all sorts of crazy things.

"Jasmine, this is just about ready. Why don't you and your friends go wash up, and then we can start dishing the food."

A dark-suited man came in the room and kissed Jasmine's mom on the forehead. Unlike Jasmine and her mom, he had dark curly hair.

"Hello boys. I'm Ted, Jasmine's father." He walked over and shook Lanny's hand, then mine. "I hear you have some sort of adventure planned?"

My eyes cut to Jasmine's, questioning her non-verbally about what she might have told him.

"Daddy," she cooed. "I told you it's a secret."

He held up his hands in mock surrender. "My lips are sealed." He twisted his fingers in front of his closed mouth as if locking his lips shut with a key.

After dinner, Jasmine, Lanny, and I convened in the dining room. Lanny pulled the official Sasquatch Hunters of Washington, Inc. notebook out of his Spider-Man backpack and laid it on the table. I produced my grandfather's night vision scope, which caused everyone to ooh and ahh. I wasn't sure what Gramps would do if he found out I'd taken it, and I didn't want to know. I told the crew no one was allowed to touch the scope except for me. If anything happened to it, I didn't want to drag them into the mix. I'd need to take the punishment all by myself.

Jasmine reached into her jeans pocket and removed something, palming it while sliding her thumb into a loop. Her face looked triumphant as she opened and closed her fist creating a clicking sound. She opened her hand to reveal a yellow wooden circle attached to a blue one forming a clamshell. The top piece had an indentation where she rested her middle fingertip.

"Are those castets?" Lanny stared in awe.

"Cast-A-nets."

"Castanets," he repeated after her. "Can I try?"

Jasmine nodded and handed them to him. He fumbled with them for a minute, so she helped him position his fingers. His first snap brought a huge smile to his face, followed by a cacophony of clacking. He clicked and clacked and clacked and clicked.

She grabbed them back, giving him an exasperated look. "Good grief, Lanny, keep it together."

He gave a sheepish smile in return.

"I'm gonna go pop the popcorn. I'll be right back." She skipped down the hallway to the kitchen.

Lanny turned to look at me. "Do you really think there's anything out there? Or are you just humoring her so you can hang around a pretty, popular girl?"

My face felt warm, and I hoped it didn't show. "I don't know what's out there, but I do believe Jasmine saw something. Maybe it was a cat, or a raccoon, or a man living in the woods. Maybe it was an as-yet-undiscovered primate. All I know is, if I can prove Bigfoot exists, I'll become famous, and maybe…" My voice trailed off. I stopped myself before I revealed too much.

"Maybe what?" Lanny asked.

"Nothing," I muttered.

"This isn't just about you, you know," Lanny said. "You aren't doing this alone, and if we discover Bigfoot, we should all get the credit." He circled his index fingers in the air to indicate inclusion of everyone.

Jasmine walked in the room holding the steaming fresh-from-the-microwave bag of popcorn. "Of course, we'll all get the credit. That's what it means to be part of a team. We're the Three Musketeers of Bigfoot hunting." She flipped her amber hair over her right shoulder. "Right?" Her expression dared me to contradict her.

"Right," I said. "I didn't mean it wasn't a group effort. It's just when I started this a year ago, I was doing it on my own and for my own reasons. I never imagined having partners, but now that I have them, I'm grateful, especially since it means I don't have to go into the woods alone."

"I'm kinda nervous," Lanny admitted.

"Me too," Jasmine said. "I'm the one who already experienced something scary out there. Honestly, I can't believe I'm going back, but I need to know what I saw." She rolled her shoulders into a determined posture.

"It's very brave of all of us." I hesitated. "I have a confession to make." They both looked at me expectantly. "This is my first night expedition."

"What?" they both yelled simultaneously.

I held up my hands. "Hey! I never claimed otherwise."

"Well, you certainly gave the impression you were an experienced squatch hunter. What was all that talk and the field observation notebook stuff?" Lanny's face scrunched into a look of dismay and distrust.

"Yeah!" Jasmine was angry. "I only told you about what happened out there because Lanny made it sound like you knew what you were doing."

"I do know what I'm doing. I've done a ton of research, but I've never had a chance to go out at night. When I lived in Florida, there was no place nearby where I could search. I've only been in Washington for a few months."

"I should have known a couple weeks ago when you let me come with you to explore the woods next to Foreman Lake. I asked what we were supposed to do first and you said 'observe.'" Lanny made air quotes. "You had no idea what you were doing, did you?"

"Yes, it was my first actual expedition…"

Both Lanny and Jasmine gave frustrated yells in response to my admission.

"However," I held my hands up to calm them down. "I've done my research, and I do know someone who's an actual eyewitness."

"Duh," Jasmine said.

"I didn't mean you."

They each eyed me with skepticism.

"You can't tell anyone." My warning elicited a

dramatic eyeroll from Jasmine.

"That's already been established. Everything that happens needs to stay in the circle of trust, just the three of us. So, tell us, who's your secret eyewitness?" She crossed her arms.

"My grandfather."

They stared at me with intense interest.

"My grandfather had a squatch encounter a few years ago." I let out a large breath.

"What kind of encounter?" Lanny asked.

"Pretty similar to Jasmine's."

Her eyes widened in surprise. "What do you mean? He saw a Bigfoot in the woods by the school too?"

"No, he was out on the Olympic Peninsula. That's what got me interested in Bigfoot hunting in the first place. We were camping a couple summers ago and he told me a Sasquatch once came to the edge of his campsite at the very same park. He described similar smells and sounds to what Jasmine experienced. He talked about golden eyes and said the creature just stood there not doing anything, just watching. After a few minutes he just left."

"That seems kind of anti-cli...climtatic. Climitic."

Lanny struggled to find the right word.

"Climactic." Jasmine and I spoke in unison.

"Right, anticlimactic. No 'ooga booga' sounds? No chasing? No throwing rocks?"

I had the feeling Lanny had watched a lot of TV shows about Bigfoot.

"No, none of that. Scientists who are willing to entertain the idea of an unknown ape in the Pacific Northwest say the idea he would act like a monster isn't realistic."

"Or she," Jasmine said.

"Or she what?" I asked.

"You said he wouldn't act like a monster, but from everything I've read, there are as many girl Bigfoot sightings as boys. Like the famous video of the Bigfoot walking…that was a girl," she said.

"How do they know it was a girl?" Lanny asked.

"She had…girl parts," Jasmine said.

This caused Lanny to dissolve into laughter. He pounded his fist on the table. "Girl parts!"

"Either way," I said. "We aren't dealing with some B-movie horror creature. It's a primate, and a smart one at that. From what I understand, most of the time people wouldn't know they were there. They would rather quietly observe than interact."

Lanny's eyes were wide. "Well let's hope he—or she—decides not to observe too closely tonight. I don't want to have to explain to my parents when they pick me up why I peed my pants at dinner."

Into the Squatchy Woods

After dinner we zipped up our jackets, loaded our gear, and headed outside with an admonition from Jasmine's parents to be cautious and safely back by nine. I had the feeling they were humoring us, not believing a legendary creature might be living in the woods near their posh, gated mansion. I didn't blame them. If I didn't know better, I'd have thought the same.

Not to say I completely believed Jasmine had seen a Sasquatch. Most of the time, cryptid sightings could be chalked up to misidentification and active imaginations. Jasmine struck me as having the latter, but she definitely saw something out there that had scared her. Besides, this was good practice for my next camping trip to the peninsula with Gramps.

In early October, the Puget Sound region often experienced warm fall days followed by crisp nights. The afternoon had been too warm for a jacket, but since the sun had set, I was glad I'd worn one. The autumn breeze rustled the remaining leaves, which barely clung to their branches. In a couple weeks those trees would be completely bare. The moon hung full and low in the sky. Gramps called it a harvest moon. It gave an orange glow and an extra spooky vibe to an already spooky adventure.

It took us about ten minutes to reach the edge of the park and the path that led into the woods. The three of us stood, unmoving.

Lanny looked at me. "So, what now?"

My mouth twisted to the left as I contemplated what it would take to muster the courage to take a step forward. I took a deep breath and turned to Jasmine. "Are you sure you want to do this?"

I was almost hoping she'd back out so I wouldn't have to go in there, but I wouldn't look like a 'fraidy cat either. She'd never let me live it down and I didn't even want to think about what Michael Blackwell would do if he found out I'd gotten all the way to the edge and then chickened out first.

Jasmine's brows scrunched together, and her lips pursed. She squared her shoulders and lifted her chin in defiance of her fear. "Come on, boys. Let's do this." She marched forward.

I should've known she'd be the bravest of all of us.

With Jasmine leading the way, I motioned for Lanny to fall in behind her, while I took the rear position. I'd have felt really bad if anything happened to him on my watch, so the safest place for him seemed to be sandwiched between us.

I spotted a three-foot-long branch that had broken off and fallen onto the path. I picked it up and showed it to the others.

"I'm bringing this stick. That way we can do tree knocks."

Jasmine took the branch from me and examined it. "What are tree knocks?"

Lanny piped up, "Oh, I know! Like on that show, where they bang sticks against the trees. It's how Bigfeet like to communicate with each other."

He grabbed the stick from Jasmine, wildly swung it around, and whacked it against a rhododendron bush. Several leaves fell to the ground in protest. I retrieved it from him before he accidentally swatted Jasmine or me.

"Is it Bigfeet or Bigfoots?" she asked.

"I've said it both ways. I could be wrong, but I think it's like deer. Whether it's one deer or two deer, it's still just deer. Same with Bigfoot. One Bigfoot, two Bigfoot," I said.

"Red Bigfoot, blue Bigfoot." Lanny laughed at his own joke.

The road that separated the school from the park intersected with a busier road, and the sound of occasional passing cars gave me some reassurance that help was not too far away if we needed it.

Jasmine's stride was slow and measured. There was a loud crackling whenever she landed on one of the many dead fallen branches covering the trail. Each step took us further into darkness and further from the lights and sounds of civilization. None of us said a word for several minutes. It was the longest I'd ever known Lanny to be quiet. Jasmine either, for that matter. At the call of a hooting owl, Jasmine froze in her tracks. We all held our breath until we couldn't any longer. Jasmine tilted her head to listen and, hearing no sound, began to walk forward again.

Lanny's flashlight bounced up and down with each dip and crest of the trail. I had a feeling his nerves also contributed to the erratic shining. About a hundred yards in, we came to the giant maple tree Jasmine had described the day she'd hired me. There was a shadowy spot that looked like an opening in the trunk covered by a tarp. There were items I couldn't make out on the ground, probably garbage. Jasmine was right. It looked like someone had been living there.

"I'm gonna try a tree knock to see if we get a response."

I whacked the stick against the maple. It made a modest thumping sound.

"Do it again!" Lanny clapped his hands with delight.

Once again, I smacked the branch against the side of the tree. We all stopped to listen, but there wasn't any audible response.

I pulled the night scope out of my backpack. I didn't really know how to use it, and I wasn't even sure it worked without the rifle. The person I knew would have the answer was the one person I couldn't ask because I'd taken it without his permission. I put the scope up to my left eye like a pirate with a spyglass. For the most part, all I saw was darkness. Turning to face Jasmine, I could see her phone glowing in her pocket. Titling my head back, the treetops gave way to a sky full of stars, which seemed brighter than normal. I brought my head back to level and began scanning the area.

"Do you see anything?" Lanny was breathless.

"Not yet," I said in a whisper. "The stars glow and Jasmine's phone glows every once in a while, but so far the woods just look dark."

"Snapchat," said Jasmine.

"What?"

"My phone keeps going off from Snapchat notifications."

"Well, maybe you could turn your phone off for now. It's distracting." My tone was hushed but insistent.

"And risk not being able to call for help? Not gonna happen," she hissed.

Lanny pulled out his notebook and began writing something, using the crook of his neck to hold the flashlight in place so he could see.

"What are you writing?" I asked.

"Observations."

"Observations of what? We haven't seen anything yet."

"Observations of you and Jasmine. So far, I've written Jasmine gets a lot of Snapchat notifications, and you talk like you're brave, but I think you're as scared as I am. Also, I wrote what you both are wearing."

I rolled my eyes but didn't bother lecturing him on what it was he was supposed to be keeping track of.

"Do you think someone lives here?" Jasmine asked.

"It kind of looks that way, but I find it hard to imagine a Sasquatch setting up a tarp to make a tent. I mean, he couldn't just go to the hardware store and pick one up, even if he knew how to make it. I could see him huddling in the tree hole, though. Not a large adult male, but a juvenile or a female." I said these things with more authority and certainty than I possessed, but somehow it brought me a sense of control and calm.

"Do you mean a naughty Bigfoot?"

Jasmine and I both turned to look at Lanny.

"Why are you looking at me that way? I thought juvenile meant you got into trouble. That's how my parents always use that word."

I chuckled. "That's a juvenile delinquent. A juvenile

simply means it's not full-grown yet."

"Ohhhh. I get it now."

I wasn't sure he really did.

We stood motionless, waiting for the bushes to indicate something hiding in them, or for a howl. Anything, really. After about twenty minutes of silence, I was about to open my mouth to call it quits for the night when there was a crack of a branch further into the woods. The three of us looked at each other, our eyes so wide we didn't need the night scope to see the whites of them in the moonlight.

My fingers fumbled as I attempted to locate the scope. Nerves got the best of me, though, because as I pulled it out, hands shaking, I dropped it on the ground. The tinkling of shattered glass filled me with even more dread. My grandfather was going to kill me. As I reached down to pick up the certainly broken equipment, a guttural grunt came from the same direction as the twig snap.

I popped to my feet, threw the scope in my backpack, and signaled to Jasmine and Lanny to start running. Jasmine was surprisingly fast, but Lanny's little legs struggled to keep up. I grabbed him by the hand and pulled him along. We made it to the park but kept running. We got to the sidewalk but kept running. We didn't stop running until we reached Jasmine's gate.

Our ten-minute walk to the park took half the time in return. My side ached, and I was having trouble catching my breath. I bent over to rest. Even though Lanny couldn't run fast, he didn't seem winded at all. Jasmine walked in circles with her arms over her head.

"What are you doing?" I asked.

"My soccer coach says putting your hands on your head helps you to not hyperventilate."

She entered a code into the call box and the gate opened.

We walked around the corner to her house, arriving just before nine. Lanny's parents were already waiting for him in the driveway. Jasmine and I waved goodbye to him, promising to talk on Monday. As their car drove away, I caught a glimpse of Lanny's traumatized face through the back-seat window.

I didn't bother looking at the scope to see the extent of the damage. I said a quick goodbye to Jasmine, hopped on my bike, and rode home with a heavy, thumping heart.

A Betrayal of
Gigantopithecal Proportion

I managed to make it through the weekend without Mom questioning me too much about what had happened at Jasmine's house or Gramps questioning me about the missing rifle scope. I didn't think he'd be using it very soon, so I hoped I had time to earn enough money to repair or replace it. I wasn't sure if it was repairable or how much one of those things cost. My ten dollar per week allowance wasn't going to be enough—of that I felt certain.

I decided I'd need to get actual paying clients. The question was, where did one acquire clients in search of mythical bipedal apes who trusted the amateur sleuthing ability of two sixth graders and a third-grade prodigy and who also had the ability to pay for our services?

At breakfast Saturday morning I considered asking my mom for an increase in my allowance, but she looked tired and distracted. The last thing I wanted to do was add to her already heavy burden.

"Are you okay, Mom?"

Gramps gave her a questioning look with raised eyebrows, which she returned with a grimace. I watched this silent conversation play out, waiting to see the outcome and who would win the stand-off. When my grandfather sighed and went back to reading his newspaper, I knew Mom had won.

"I'm fine, Jake. I'm just worn out from a long week."

Her tone told me that was the end of the conversation.

When everyone had finished their Dutch babies, I offered to do the dishes. It was part of my campaign to get a raise. Mom gave me a side-eye look as if she suspected I was up to something but decided not to press the issue since she was getting unexpected cooperation. She left me alone in the kitchen and headed upstairs.

When I'd finished drying the baking dish, I opened

a few cupboards looking for where it was supposed to go. I found a space in a cupboard up high and lifted the glass pan onto the second shelf by standing on my tiptoes. I used my fingers to nudge the dish into place and shut the cabinet. As I came down onto flat feet, I accidentally bumped the stack of mail piled next to the phone. Several envelopes, advertising flyers, and catalogs cascaded onto the floor. As I bent over and began to gather the papers, an envelope caught my eye. The bottom had been ripped as if opened upside down.

The envelope, with my mother's name handwritten in the center, had an Orlando return address and a two-week-old postmark.

I knew I wasn't supposed to read other people's mail. I was pretty sure it was a federal crime, not to mention something that would have most definitely gotten me grounded if I got caught.

It was just such a strange thing to get handwritten letters, especially from Orlando. I wondered if maybe Mrs. Langford had sent it. Suddenly, I felt overcome with homesickness for our old apartment and our nice, old neighbor lady who smelled like the doctor's office and chocolate chip cookies. I was also overcome with curiosity.

Contained within the envelope was a short note.

Bianca,

You can't keep me from him forever. A son has the right to know his father, and a father has the right to know his son.

It wasn't signed at the bottom. Only the initial C had been scrawled below those two unbelievable sentences. My heart began beating so fast that I thought it might jump right out of my chest. My hands shook so hard that the letter fluttered like hummingbird wings. My eyes scanned the two short phrases over and over as if I'd maybe I'd misread them, or I'd missed something which would make the note not say what I thought it said. Maybe if I read it again, I'd see how I'd misunderstood, or new information might suddenly appear, which would make it all make sense.

No matter how many times I read the words, they said the same thing.

This had to be from my father. My father, who clearly wanted to see me. My father, who my mom had apparently been keeping away from me. How could she have done that to me? She'd known how desperate I'd been to know who he was, to know him, because I'd told her.

It was the day she told me we were moving to Washington. I'd gotten upset and started crying. I told her I was worried if we left Orlando, he'd never be able to find me.

"I'm not moving!"

"Jake." She sighed one of the deepest sighs I'd ever heard…and that was saying a lot because she sighed all the time.

"Where is he?"

"I don't know."

Now it turned out she'd had all the answers all along. Well, at least for the past two weeks. She'd said nothing to me about it.

I didn't know what to do with the information. I wondered if I should confront her or my grandfather, who must have known about the letter based on the looks he'd been giving her at breakfast. I would definitely get in trouble for reading her mail, but now that I had, it felt completely justified.

I didn't know whether to cry or yell. I wanted to do both. My stomach felt queasy, and my hands were shaking at the thought of confronting my mom. At the same time, I had butterflies because I was closer to knowing about my dad than I'd ever been in my entire life. He wanted to see me.

My eyes filled with tears.

My dad wanted me.

My dad wanted me, and my mom was keeping me from him. Why would she do that? I wanted to believe she had good reasons, but I couldn't think of any.

The hardest part of the whole thing was the two people I would normally talk to about my feelings, Mom and Gramps, were the last two people I wanted to talk to under the circumstances. I felt betrayed by them, the people I trusted the most.

I felt terrible. My head and heart both pounded. I felt nauseated. My hands were clammy, and I felt a surge of energy like I needed to punch a heavy bag about a hundred times or run around the block. The problem was, I was so upset I thought if I started running, I may not stop until I got to Florida.

If I'd still been in Orlando, I could have talked to my buddy Chase, but I wasn't in Orlando, and Chase and I had barely talked since I'd moved. I thought about calling Jasmine but then I would have to explain to her that I didn't know who my father was, and why. I'd have to tell her my mom and Gramps had been keeping him from me all this time, even after he told them he wanted to see me. I felt too embarrassed to have her know those things, and my heart hurt too much to hear her tell me what I already knew: my life was a disaster, and my family was kind of a mess.

I panicked at the sound of footsteps on the stairs. I shoved the letter back into the envelope and tucked the envelope back into the pile of mail. I finished right as my mom walked into the kitchen. She looked at me with narrowed eyes like she sensed I'd been doing something I shouldn't have been. I wanted to return her glare, but I didn't. I needed time to sort out my thoughts about the situation before I confronted her with what I knew. I needed to hone my investigative skills to solve two mysteries now...the mystery of my long-lost father and the mystery of what had frightened Jasmine in the woods across from Hawthorne Elementary.

12

A Simple Squatchy Plan

On Monday at lunch recess, Sasquatch Hunters convened near the hopscotch court. I'd spent the previous forty-eight hours processing my thoughts after discovering not only that A) my father was alive, but also B) he wanted to see me. The result of all that thinking was that I'd solidified my resolve to figure out what inhabited those woods.

My father had sent the letter to my mom at Gramps' house, so he knew where we were. What he probably didn't know was that I wanted to meet him too. If I used Jasmine's phone to post videos on YouTube and

TikTok, and then I called the newspapers and TV stations with proof I'd discovered Bigfoot, my story would be everywhere, all over the world. Then I could tell my father I wanted him to come find me and he'd see it. I'd spent much of Saturday night imagining the look on my mother's face when my father showed up to claim me. It would serve her right.

I also felt less guilty about breaking my grandfather's scope. A broken scope was nothing compared to breaking someone's trust, as I felt he'd done by keeping information about my father from me. I still wanted to get it repaired, though, so I brought up the idea of how to market Sasquatch Hunters to a broader customer base than just the Hawthorne Elementary playground.

"What exactly did you have in mind?" Jasmine asked. "I want to be involved, but I do have a reputation to protect."

"Me too," said Lanny.

Jasmine and I both laughed at his statement, which he didn't seem to appreciate.

"I'm not sure what our next step should be. Every business needs clients, and we already know there's a market for our services. Jasmine's experience and my grandfather's encounter can't be the only ones. Neither one of you wanted to talk about it for fear of being ridiculed, but you still wanted answers about what you saw. We can provide those answers to people like you, for a small fee."

"It can't be too small. It has to be split three ways."

"I know, Jasmine. Plus, I have to replace or repair my grandfather's scope before he discovers it's broken. That's part of the cost of doing business."

"How much is that gonna cost?" Lanny pulled out his notebook. "I'm trying to keep track of expenses. So far, all I've got is twenty-five cents for the pencil I lost in the woods when we ran out of there."

"I'm not sure yet. I'll have to get my mom to take me to Cabela's so I can find out."

"In the meantime, my mom agreed to print the materials I asked for. In addition to business cards, she's doing flyers. Maybe we could post them downtown."

"Good idea. I've also been thinking about setting up a booth at the park. The noises we heard Friday night weren't normal, and if we gave people a place to report what they've seen and heard, we might get some good feedback or even a client. Jasmine was supposed to be a paying client…until she hired herself."

"I bring a lot to the table." She said this without a hint of apology.

She was right. Between the resources her mom was willing to provide and her fervent belief in what we were trying to prove, her involvement was worth way more than the five or ten dollars I'd originally intended to charge her for my solo services.

We agreed on a plan to get the flyers printed in the next few days and have them posted around town by Friday. Since Jasmine was the only one with a cell phone, she agreed to have her number listed. She'd jot down any tips which were called in or any potential client contact info. Lanny said he'd create a budget on an Excel spreadsheet like what his father used for their household expenses. I didn't know what that was, some sort of computer program or something, but I figured having a budget might be a good idea. I'd ask Gramps for a TV tray and chair to set up in the park. I'd have to carry them on the bus in the morning, and then drag them home on foot, but if we got some action, it would totally be worth it.

Unfortunately, Jasmine had soccer practice, and Lanny had a birthday party to attend.

I'm not sure what I'd expected to happen when I put up a makeshift booth with a handwritten sign and plopped myself in the middle of Hawthorne Park advertising cryptid hunting services, but business was slow. By slow, I meant nonexistent. A couple of kids who were too young to read tried to buy my half-drunk Gatorade for a quarter. Some ladies in exercise clothes and tennis shoes speed-walked past me, offering patronizing smiles of condolence over my silly endeavor. Thankfully, I'd arrived at four-thirty, and the after-school crowd had already cleared out.

I'd been sitting there for so long that my eyelids began to get droopy. I let them rest a little longer with each blink until each blink became heavier and further between.

From a distance, footsteps grew closer, accompanied by what could only be described as a maniacal cackle. The sounds seemed to pick up speed and volume. My eyes flung open just as my clipboard flipped up from the TV tray, into the air, and crashed back down.

"Good one, Michael!" Charlie the minion cheered on his leader.

"What the heck? You almost smacked me in the face!" I hollered.

Michael picked up the clipboard before I could grab it away from him. "What do we have here? What show is this for? Are you signing up kids for the school play?"

Charlie parroted him in a similar mocking tone. "Yeah, are you gonna play Peter Pan? Get it? 'Cause you're short!"

I scrunched my face. "Who said Peter Pan is short?"

"'Cause he never grows!"

"He never grows up," I corrected.

Michael laughed the classic laugh of playground bullies all over the world. "No, Charlie, Jake's so short he'd have to play tiny little Tinker Bell!"

I shook my head. "Michael, I have no idea what you're talking about."

Michael threw the clipboard back onto the table. He pointed at what I'd written at the top of the page. "Right there. It says 'show.'"

I stared at the page for a moment before I threw my head back and burst out laughing. I'd written the acronym of Sasquatch Hunters of Washington, S.H.O.W. I just hadn't realized it spelled out a word.

Michael's eyes narrowed and he leaned in toward me. "What's so funny?"

"What's funny is you have no idea what you're talking

about." And boy, was I glad about that.

Once again, Michael's face turned a color somewhere between watermelon and eggplant. "You think you're so cool because you lived by Disney World and Jasmine's being nice to you."

I felt genuinely surprised by this statement. "You think I think I'm cool?"

"Well, you're wrong! You're not cool, and she's only being nice to you because she feels sorry for you. I'm watching you, Jake. I'm gonna find out what you're up to, and then the whole school is going to hear about it. Then maybe you'll go back to wherever it is you came from."

"Florida."

"Whatever!"

Michael stomped off, with Charlie trailing close behind. Charlie said something I couldn't quite make out, but Michael shushed him and threw one more glare over his shoulder and in my direction.

The clouds had begun to thicken. The winds picked up, blowing the remaining leaves off of trees in the process of going dormant for the winter. Just as I started to pack up for the long trudge home, Gramps arrived.

"How's business?"

I contorted my lips into a grimace. "About how you might expect. What are you doing here?"

"Well, I thought you might like a ride. I'm sure it wasn't easy dragging the table and chair over here from the school, and it's a mighty long way back to the house."

I sighed. "That would be great, thanks."

We loaded my stuff into the back of the blue van and hopped into the front.

"I'm sorry things didn't work out. It'll be better next time."

His kindness and encouragement made me feel terrible. I could no longer hold in my secret.

"I borrowed your night scope without asking, and it broke! I'm so sorry! I'll do whatever you need me to do to pay it back."

Instead of surprise, he wore an expression of compassion. "Thank you for telling me."

"That's it? That's all you have to say about it? You're not gonna yell at me?"

He chuckled. "Do you want me to yell at you? Will

that make you feel better?" He backed out of the parking spot and headed toward home.

I wriggled in the seat, my windbreaker swooshing against the leather. "Well, no, it wouldn't make me feel better. But aren't you mad at me?"

"Jake, I trust you. If you took it without asking, I'm sure you had a good reason."

That made me feel even worse. "The other night, when I went to Jasmine's for dinner, we did a night investigation. I used the scope to try and see what had made a noise, and in the chaos, the scope fell out of my hands and cracked. I'd hoped to get a new client today so I could buy you a new one."

"I'm curious, why did you feel you couldn't trust me enough to come to me directly and ask permission to borrow it? I would have said yes."

"I don't know, I guess I was scared you wouldn't want me to go. And I really wanted to go."

"I get that, but Jake, relationships are built on trust and honesty, and giving people the benefit of the doubt."

His statement hit me hard, especially considering what I'd discovered Saturday morning.

"Then why are you and mom keeping my dad from

me? Why didn't you tell me he wants to see me? Why did she hide his letter?" My voice got high with anger and nearly cracked with the tears threatening to break free.

I felt mad. It seemed like there were two sets of rules for how to treat people, one for kids and one for adults. Adults acted like they didn't have to justify their choices to their kids, but kids always had to answer for their choices. It wasn't fair.

Gramps pulled into the driveway and put the van into park. He let out a large gush of air and turned to look at me. "It's a tough situation your mom is in. My job is to support her as she tries to navigate it the best way she knows how. I've got my opinions on what she should do, sure, but in the end she's your mom, and she loves you, so you should trust she's doing what she thinks is best for you."

"I'm twelve years old. I'm not a baby anymore! I should have a say in my own life. I want to know who my father is." I could no longer hold back the tears.

Gramps rubbed the back of his neck, wincing. "I'm sorry, kiddo. The decision isn't up to me, it's up to your mother. But I'll have your back if you want to sit and talk it out with her."

"Thanks," I mumbled and wiped my eyes. I hated crying in front of people.

He was right, it wasn't his place to tell me anything my mom didn't want me to know. Still, I felt frustrated he refused to release a secret I badly wanted—no, needed—to know. It was as if I were on one side of the Grand Canyon while Gramps and Mom stood on the other. The darkness and the secrets which separated us made me feel more alone than I ever had in my entire life.

13

If You Just Believe

At four in the afternoon on the following Tuesday, the first call from the flyers came in. Lanny and I were over at Jasmine's for a strategy session. Jasmine answered the call on speakerphone so Lanny and I could hear.

"Is this Sasquatch Hunters of Washington?" The voice sounded gravelly, rumbly, deep, and mysterious.

"Yes, it is. This is Jasmine Davis. I'm co-president—"

"Vice president!" I whispered.

"Is someone else there?" asked the man.

Jasmine threw me a scowl. "Yes, sir. We're all here. How can we help you?"

The man paused before he responded. "Who is we?"

"As the flyers stated, Sasquatch Hunters of Washington, Inc. consists of myself, our founder Jake Nelson, and our assistant Lanny Mahajan."

"Executive assistant," Lanny corrected her, and she gave him an even more withering gaze than she'd given me.

"I apologize for my colleagues. Where were we, Mr., uh...I'm sorry, I didn't catch your name."

Instead of giving an answer, the man hung up.

"Look what you did! Next time I'm not putting the call on speaker."

"That was weird," I said.

"You're telling me." Lanny shuddered. "His voice reminded me of the Haunted Mansion ride at Disney World."

His statement caused me to jerk my head to look at him.

"What did I say?"

I shook my head. "Nothing. It's nothing. It couldn't be."

Jasmine swatted at me. "Hey, no holding back information from your partners."

"It's just...well..." I sighed. "For a second I wondered if it might be my dad."

"Your dad?" Lanny reared his head back. "You've never talked about your dad. I didn't even know you had a dad."

"Everybody has a dad, Lanny." Jasmine blew her hair out of her face. "The question is, why would Jake's dad be calling Sasquatch Hunters?"

"Everybody may have a dad, but I've never met mine. I recently found out he's been trying to see me. Of course, he's in Orlando, so there's no way he could have seen our flyer."

"Is that why you got that look when Lanny said he sounded like the voice from Disney World? Because he lives near there?"

"Actually, I have a suspicion my mom met him when she worked at Disney World. She played Ariel."

Jasmine's mouth gaped open. "Ariel's my favorite princess!"

"Hmm," I said. "I would have thought Jasmine, because of, well, your name."

"I like Jasmine. She's just not my favorite princess."

"You like Ariel because of your hair, don't you?" Lanny nodded and smirked in a knowing way.

She flipped her strawberry mane behind her shoulder. "Sorta, but I always liked the fact she went after what she wanted, even though everybody told her she couldn't or shouldn't. I'm a fan of other strong women."

Lanny blinked rapidly. "She was a fish who gave up her voice to kiss a boy!"

Jasmine rolled her eyes. "You don't get it, Lanny. It's okay, someday you'll understand."

Lanny mimicked her with a sour expression, bobbing his head back and forth, and mouthing, "you don't get it, Lanny."

"Can we get back to the topic at hand? How are we going to get paying clients?" I was still trying to figure out how to approach the conversation with my mom about finding the letter, and I didn't want them asking questions I wasn't yet prepared to answer.

"We haven't given the flyers a chance yet. They just went up over the weekend and we've already had our first call. Next time maybe you guys should leave the talking to me, so we don't scare them off."

"I think we should consider going back to the woods. All we proved the other night is Jasmine wasn't crazy or seeing things and someone—or something—is living out there."

"I'm good." Jasmine's voice sounded resolute but also a little wobbly. "No need to go back." She leaned against the wall and waved her hand dismissively.

Lanny nodded. "I agree with Jasmine. I've had my fill of spooky woods at night."

"Suit yourselves, but I want to know what's out there. I'm going tomorrow after school. Maybe something will show in the daylight we couldn't see in the dark. I want to look more closely at the tree and the camp someone set up. I mean, if a Sasquatch is living there, where would it go during the day while kids are playing at the park? We don't even know how far back that path goes or where it leads."

"I know where it leads. My dad and I flew a drone with a camera attached over the woods once," Lanny said.

"Oh yeah? What did you see?"

"Mostly just the tops of trees. It gets pretty thick, but it leads to a clearing, sort of. It's, what do you call it? Not a swamp, really. I think my dad called them wetlands.

He said no one can build houses there because that's where special birds and stuff live."

Jasmine's eyes grew wide. "Wetlands! Everybody knows Bigfoot likes wetlands. It provides water and food, and people can't really go there because it's protected by the government and they can't walk around without sinking into the marsh. It's practically like quicksand."

I nodded my head. "This is huge news, Lanny. Any chance your dad still has the footage? I'd like to see it."

"Me too!"

"I'll try. I haven't exactly explained to him what we're up to. He thinks it's a study group and I'm helping you guys with your homework."

We both stared back at him. "We're three years older than you."

"Highly capable." He shrugged, as if it were explanation enough.

Jasmine huffed in indignation, but I thought he had a point. He probably knew more than me about a lot of things, especially my least favorite subject, math.

"What if you said it was for a science project? Tell him I've got to do a report on ecology." I really wanted to see that video.

"I can try. He's in New Jersey visiting family until tomorrow night, but maybe we can have a viewing party at my house on Friday night."

"That's a good idea. Let us know. In the meantime, I'm still planning on going to the woods tomorrow. You guys can come or not, it's up to you."

"I'm out," Lanny said. "I have to ride the bus home tomorrow. My mom is making biryani because it's my dad's favorite, but it takes forever so she won't be able to pick me up."

Jasmine pulled her mouth to one side. "Fine, I'll go with you, but the second I hear even one heavy breath or cracking branch, I'm out of there."

"Scaredy-cat."

I said this as if I were completely unafraid and wouldn't run away if I caught even a whiff of skunkiness. I was totally and completely bluffing.

Something Squatchy This Way Comes

Tuesday afternoon it rained. This wasn't a big surprise. It was autumn in the Pacific Northwest, so basically our default weather. Sunny days were the exception in the fall and winter. I wore my most comfortable tennis shoes since I'd have to walk home after the expedition back into the woods. The last time I had to walk home I'd come to realize just how far it was, and my feet were not happy with me. I also had on a warm jacket my mother insisted I bring, despite the fact that the fluffy down black coat made me look like an overly toasted— aka burnt—version of the Stay Puft Marshmallow Man from *Ghostbusters*.

I felt so anxious for the end of school that several times throughout the day I found myself bouncing my knee up and down and drumming my fingers on my desk. Mr. Stevens finally had enough and yelled at me to knock it off.

The plan was for Jasmine to meet me in front of the school so we could walk to the park together. I wasn't sure if it was for convenience or because she was worried I wouldn't be able to hold my own if I ran into Michael and his little minion Charlie. It would have been humiliating for her to think I needed a bodyguard, whether true or not. Either way, being seen with the prettiest, most popular girl in school was never a bad thing and could only help boost my still-developing reputation.

When I spotted her, she was walking with Danielle, Erika, and Kayla under a giant green umbrella. She said something, and they all turned to stare at me. I felt like an animal in a zoo exhibit. Danielle leaned in and whispered something in Jasmine's ear, and even though I couldn't see her face clearly, red flushed the back of her neck. Even her scalp was pink where her strawberry hair was parted. She scrunched her shoulders to take a deep breath, before blowing it out and turning on her heel to come my way.

"What was that about? You look embarrassed. Are you embarrassed to be seen with me?"

Her face was still fuchsia. "No. It's nothing. Let's go."

I wanted to push the issue further, but she clearly didn't want to talk about it. She marched off toward the park and I hustled to catch up to her. I struggled to keep up because her legs were longer than mine, but she had an umbrella, and I only had a hood to cover my dark hair that curled into ringlets when it got wet, so staying close was necessary.

Ms. Hinkle manned the crosswalk, as usual, carrying a bright orange flag and wearing a matching vest. She looked between Jasmine and me and gave me a little smile, like she knew a secret. I figured she felt happy for me that I'd found a friend following the whole Michael phone debacle on the first day.

Since the rain fell heavily, there were few people at the park. A couple of unhappy-looking moms sat at the picnic bench under cover while their children scooted down slick slides, which became muddier by the minute. The boys who usually played football on the grass field were nowhere to be seen and I breathed a sigh of relief. For the first time since I'd moved to Washington, I felt happy it was raining. One day I'd have to deal with

Michael once and for all, but I was perfectly content for today to not be that day.

When we'd reached the edge of the woods, Jasmine finally spoke. "Do you smell that?"

I inhaled deeply. "What am I trying to identify?" I thought maybe she smelled the tell-tale skunky squatch odor. I had a bit of a cold, so my sniffer wasn't working too well.

"Just the rain on the pine trees. I think it's one of the best smells in the world."

I had to agree with her. When it rained in Orlando it smelled like swamp and flowers. It was not so fresh and clean as Washington.

We began walking the path into the forest.

"I forgot to tell you, I ran into Michael and Charlie the other day when I was here with my Sasquatch Hunters booth."

Jasmine turned her head to look at me. "Yikes. How did that go? Did they know what you were doing there?"

"Apparently not. I don't think they saw the sign I'd taped to the front of the table. I had a clipboard with a sheet for people to put their contact information, but he thought I was trying to sign people up for the school play."

She stopped walking and scrunched her nose. "Where did he get that idea?"

I stopped next to her. "You know I hate to give Michael credit for anything, but because of him, I realized something. I hadn't written out the name of the company on the paper, just the acronym S.H.O.W. If you take the first letter of each part of our name, Sasquatch Hunters of Washington, it spells show!"

Jasmine blinked a couple times and then laughed. "You're right! I like that! Sasquatch Hunters of Washington, where we'll show you proof Bigfoot exists."

I laughed. "We'd better find some proof then."

We once again trudged along the path.

"Hey, Jasmine, do you want to talk about what happened back there? With your friends, I mean."

She stopped, looking momentarily confused until recognition passed across her face. "Oh. Not really." She began walking again.

"I thought partners didn't keep secrets."

She gave a look of irritation at having her own words thrown back at her. "Some things, personal things, can be kept private."

"What's the big deal? Why are you acting so weird about it?"

"It's embarrassing."

"You don't have to be embarrassed with me. We're friends."

"It's sort of...about you." Once again, her neck flushed to a hot pink color like a flamingo.

My stomach lurched like I was riding an express elevator down a hundred levels in mere seconds. "What do you mean it's about me?"

She didn't stop, and she didn't answer.

"Jasmine, I have the right to know what people are saying about me. Come on, tell me."

She came to an abrupt halt. "Shhhh."

"Jasmine!" I was losing patience.

I caught up until I stood shoulder to shoulder—well, shoulder to upper arm—with her. Gone was her furious blush. Instead, she looked paler than normal with her face totally drained of color. Her eyes were opened so wide they appeared to have increased in size. Her mouth trembled and her lips were slightly apart in the shape of a small O.

"Did you hear that?" Her voice was barely audible.

I lowered my voice to a whisper to match hers. "No, I guess I was too busy talking. What did you hear?"

"Grunt."

Drops of fat rain plopped onto the canopy of trees above us, cascading onto her umbrella and sliding off with a plink-plink onto the rocky path. The wind tapered, and the cocoon of the thick stumps and evergreen boughs surrounding us muffled the sound of the world outside the woods. To the right of us stood the giant maple with the hollowed-out trunk, but she wasn't looking there, which meant the sound had come from elsewhere.

She looked so frightened and her fear was contagious, but my strongest feeling was a need to comfort her. I reached for the hand which wasn't holding the umbrella, her right hand, and cupped it in mine. It was smaller, despite her being taller than me, and it felt damp. I didn't have time or inclination to figure out if it was from the rain or nerves.

She looked down at our hands, and then at me, with surprise. She returned her attention to the path before us.

"He's here," she murmured. "I can sense him."

I followed her gaze, scanning the horizon of shrubs and trees. A rumble sounded from about thirty feet away, kind of like an old pickup truck traveling down a gravel road. Her hand vibrated with fear and I gripped it tighter. I opened my mouth, but no sound came out. I tried again and managed to eke out a raspy "RUN!"

My command resonated like the shot of a starter pistol at the beginning of a race, prompting both of us to take off as quickly as our bodies could move.

From behind, I heard a more pronounced grunt and then a thump. A boulder about the size of a basketball landed next to me. Somehow, I managed to pick up my already lightning-fast pace. I felt pretty sure we were setting some sort of land speed record getting out of those woods. Unfortunately, no one but us was there to attest to it.

Like the last time we'd rushed out of the woods, we didn't stop when we hit the grass, running all the way to the covered picnic area. The moms who were sitting at the table gossiping looked surprised at our frenzied arrival, but we were too out of breath to explain.

What would we have said to them anyway? Hey, just so you know, there might be a Bigfoot over there, so you probably want to keep an eye on your kids. They would have looked at us even more suspiciously than they already were in the moment. Jasmine bent over, her hands on her knees, trying to catch her breath.

After a few minutes and some slow breathing exercises, we just stared at each other.

"Welp," I said. "That definitely was something."

She nodded her head.

"Are you glad you came?"

She shook her head.

"No?"

"No. That was terrifying."

"What do you think we should do?"

"Call the police."

At the word police, the mothers looked alarmed.

"Is everything okay?" one of the women asked.

We looked again at each other, unsure what to say. Jasmine cocked her eyebrow at me and shrugged her shoulders.

Finally, I said, "There's someone, or something, in the woods who shouldn't be there."

The women immediately began calling their children away from the play structure.

"We're leaving, and I think you should as well. It's probably people doing drugs," one of the moms said, whispering the last word.

I didn't see the point in arguing with her. They bundled up bookbags and lunch boxes and ushered their kids to cars parked on the street adjacent to the park.

Jasmine pulled out her phone.

"What are you doing?"

"Calling the police, like I said."

"Wait! If we call the police and they find him, we won't get famous for discovering Bigfoot, the policemen will."

"If I don't, we'll probably become famous for being the first known victims of a Sasquatch attack. What's your obsession with being famous, anyway?"

I felt too embarrassed to explain about my plan to get my father's attention. "I just don't want other people taking credit for our discovery."

"We'll still get credit. I'll make sure of it." She dialed the phone. "Hi, my name is Jasmine Davis and I'm at Hawthorne Park across from the elementary school.

My friend and I just had a dangerous encounter with a madman in the woods." She listened quietly. "Yes, we'll wait here." She hung up.

"Why did you say that?"

"Because," she said in her most *duh* voice. "If I told them we just saw Bigfoot they'd think it was a prank call. Come to think of it, maybe I should've called animal control instead."

I Mustache You
Some Questions

Only about ten or fifteen minutes had passed when a Hawthorne police car arrived at the park. The officers—a tall, thin, dark-skinned woman with black hair pulled into a bun at the nape of her neck and a stocky bald guy with a thick dark gray mustache like a walrus—walked over to us.

"Are you the ones who called in the incident?" asked the female officer.

"That was me," said Jasmine.

"What were you kids doing back there anyway?" This time the question came from the mustache. "You'd better not have been neckin'."

"Neckin'?" I had no idea what he meant. "Do you mean knocking?"

The woman rolled her eyes at her partner. "Geez, Carl, it's not 1955." She turned her attention back to us. Her brown eyes were serious but kind. "He means were you kissing?"

I blinked rapidly, so horrified by the question I couldn't find words.

Jasmine sure could, though, and they didn't make me feel any better. "Eww! Gross! No way!"

Both officers looked at me with pity.

The woman, who seemed to be in charge even though she looked younger than the mustache, said, "Can you tell us what you witnessed?"

I felt too mortified by Jasmine's annihilation of my ego to respond.

She jumped in with a fib. "We were working on a science project. We're studying local ecology and were collecting leaves and pine cones."

Officer Mustache—Carl—guffawed. "Well then, where are your specimens?" His tone sounded mocking, as if he didn't believe her.

"We dropped them when we were practically attacked!" Jasmine gave him her most withering look.

I felt vindicated to see I wasn't the only one undone by it. Officer Mustache shut his yap right quick.

"What do you mean by attacked?" asked the female officer, whose nametag read Barnes.

"There's a big maple tree a little way into the woods. Rumor has it, kids go there to party or whatever, or homeless people live there. There's a lot of trash, but we found no one at the tree when we got there. Further ahead, though, someone made loud scary noises, like they were trying to frighten us away. It worked."

"Kids, you know it's a crime to make a false police report, right?" Officer Mustache's voice held a stern warning. "Make sure your statement is completely accurate. Don't add details to make it more exciting. It sounds as if you were someplace you shouldn't be, probably doing stuff you shouldn't be doing, and you got spooked, but you can't go calling the cops just 'cause."

"We aren't making it up!" I yelled. "And we weren't doing anything wrong. Someone—or something—is out there and it threw a big rock at us to get us to leave."

"Okay, okay." Officer Barnes attempted to calm the

situation. "We'll go check it out."

Officer Mustache didn't like that idea, but he followed her across the field anyway.

"I want to be her when I grow up," breathed Jasmine, her voice filled with awe.

"Who? Officer Barnes?"

"Yeah. Did you see how she handled the other policeman? She's in charge and there's nothing he can do about it. I want to be in charge." Her face glowed with admiration.

I had every reason to believe that if Jasmine Davis wanted to be in charge, she would be.

The weather got stormier, and we huddled together beneath her umbrella just under the eaves where rain cascaded like a waterfall and wind whipped around us. After a few minutes we heard some shouting. We looked at each other wide-eyed, wondering if we were about to witness an historic event.

Would they shoot it? Would they drag it out of the woods like a bear about to be made into a rug? Would they call the news? Or the president? Would they steal the credit or hoist us onto their shoulders like a baseball player who had hit the walk-off home run in the World Series?

The laurel shrubs at the entrance to the path rustled and swayed, not just from the wind. Officer Mustache appeared first, followed by a large figure—easily six foot four inches—with its broad shoulders hunched forward. Officer Barnes followed, grasping its arm.

"Jake?" Jasmine said.

"Yeah."

"Does Bigfoot usually wear a yellow rain slicker?"

Officer Barnes, the Mustache, and the giant banana slogged toward us through the mud and wet grass. Every step closer caused my heart to sink. This wasn't a Bigfoot. It was just a large man in a raincoat. There would be no credit for the discovery because there was no discovery. There would be no media coverage, no call to or from the president.

Officer Mustache wore a smirk so big it was actually visible underneath the hairy slug which sat upon his upper lip. Officer Barnes had a serious expression on her face, and I feared she was angry. Whether at us or the man in custody, I couldn't quite tell.

A gust of wind yanked the hood of the slicker from the head of the figure, causing both Jasmine and me to gasp.

A man with wet dark curly hair looked back at us.

I found his expression difficult to read. He seemed irritated but also slightly regretful. He locked eyes with me. I looked closer. They were hazel like mine. It was the strangest sensation, because it felt like looking in a mirror at my own eyes.

Who Do You Think You Are?

"Is this the man who attacked you?" asked Officer Barnes.

"I didn't attack anyone!" The man's deep and raspy voice grumbled. His voice sounded frustrated but not menacing, and also an awful lot like the man who'd called Jasmine's phone looking for Sasquatch Hunters.

"It's hard to tell," said Jasmine. "We didn't actually see it…I mean him."

Officer Mustache scowled. "You called us out here claiming there was a wild man. Now you're telling us you never even laid eyes on the guy?" He kicked the dirt with the pointy end of his shoe, but the rain had turned it to mud so it got lodged in place. He struggled to pull the toe of his boot out of the muck, which he did, eventually, accompanied by a large suction sound as it released.

"We heard grunting sounds, like a gorilla, and it— he—threw a big rock at us as we ran away! What should we have done?"

Officer Barnes eyed me curiously. "It's interesting. Both of you said it before correcting yourselves to say him. What's that all about?"

Jasmine and I looked at each other.

I was about to open my mouth to respond when the man in the yellow rain slicker bellowed, "Are you gonna detain me or are you gonna let me go?"

It was Officer Barnes and the Mustache's turn to exchange meaningful glances.

"Sir, can you please state your name?" She looked at the man in the yellow slicker. She nodded to Officer Mustache, who pulled out a pad, his pen poised to take notes.

The man looked sadly at me. "My name is Clifton Blake." He scanned my face as if searching for a hint of recognition. When there was none, he continued. "I live in Orlando, Florida."

Suddenly it was as if I were on the tilt-a-whirl at the carnival. Though I stood still, the world around me started spinning. His words echoed in my mind, which was trying to connect dots, look for resemblances between us, and make sense of the words coming out of his mouth. Did those words mean what I thought they meant?

I slumped to the ground, not even caring about the fact that my mother was going to kill me for getting mud all over my clothes. Laundry would be the least of her concerns when I dragged home my long-lost father.

"Son, are you okay? You look pretty pale." Officer Barnes reached down to touch my shoulder.

"Are you...are you my father?" The words came out in a rush, along with a tidal wave of feelings. I burst into tears when he nodded his head. I caught a glimpse of Jasmine's shocked face, and I felt horrified to have her witness me crying, but I couldn't stop so instead I buried my face in my muddy hands.

The Mustache appeared befuddled by the whole scene. "Wait. You're his father? But he didn't know that? And you live in Florida, but you're here? And you followed him into the forest and grunted at him, throwing rocks at your own kid to scare him away?"

Officer Barnes interrupted his questions. "Officer Adamczyk, we appreciate the recap, but perhaps Mr. Blake would like to give us his explanation."

The man...Mr. Blake...my father...gave a sheepish look. "Fifteen years ago, I met the most beautiful girl I'd ever seen walking toward me in a long hallway holding a giant head under her arm."

Everyone reacted in different ways to his statement. Officer Barnes's forehead crinkled, the Mustache's mustache twitched, Jasmine's mouth formed into a grimace, and my head jerked back like a dog on a leash.

Clifton Blake laughed at our varying responses. "She was holding the head of Smee, Captain Hook's sidekick from Peter Pan. It was my first day working as a character at Disney World and she was getting ready to go out into the park. She brushed past me with her long shiny dark hair flowing behind her. For me, it was love at first sight. For her, it...wasn't." He paused, presumably remembering the rejection, as evidenced by the frown on his face.

Officer Mustache interrupted. "Look, we can't stay here all day. Mind speeding up story time?"

"I've had a dozen years to think about how I would tell this story to my son someday, and that day is finally here. Maybe you could show a little compassion." He chastised the Mustache before looking at me again with those sad hazel eyes. "Look, Jake, I messed up. I hurt your mom pretty badly. I understand why she cut me out of your lives. There hasn't been a single day I haven't thought about you and been angry with myself for ruining everything."

Everyone stood silent. I was speechless, trying to absorb what he'd said. I didn't feel a lot, other than just sad. Sad for my mom, sad for me, and, surprisingly, sad for this man I'd never met who made some dumb mistakes which had cost all of us the chance to be a family.

"W-when did you find out about me?"

"Your mom called me after you were born. She did let me see you once, but at that meeting she told me the two of you were better off without me and asked me to leave you both alone."

"How could she do that? How could she make my decision for me?"

"Moms have to make a lot of difficult choices for their kids," said Officer Barnes softly. "We do the best we can with the information we have."

Clifton Blake nodded. "Kiddo, I don't blame her, and you shouldn't either."

Officer Barnes gave a sympathetic look. "This all sounds like stuff you guys need to talk through with the boy's mother. In the meantime, can you tell us what happened today?"

"Oh, yeah. Sorry. So, I've been in the area for a couple weeks, getting the lay of the land, scoping out the school and the park and stuff. I'd parked over there." He indicated a black car. "I saw these two headed across from the school in the rain. I was worried they might be up to no good, like me at their age, so I followed them in. I hid behind trees and bushes. The next thing I knew, they were running out, so I hid behind a big oak tree. I waited for them to leave so I could come out without being seen, but then you guys showed up and I didn't know what to do. I knew it looked pretty bad." He turned to face me. "This isn't how I wanted us to meet for the first time, with me detained by the police, looking like a criminal. I promise, I'm not a bad guy. I just want a chance to know my son."

At the words my son my chest constricted. I'd never heard anyone refer to me that way before. I didn't even know how I felt about it, but I knew I felt something.

"I think we can release you," said Officer Barnes. "But I'd like you two kids to call your parents to come pick you up. We'd give you a ride, but it can be pretty traumatizing to see your child brought home in a police car." She pulled out a key and unlocked the handcuffs.

Clifton Blake rubbed his now-free wrists.

Jasmine pulled out her cell phone and handed it to me. I slowly pushed each button, dread mounting inside me knowing this wasn't going to be a fun conversation. When my mother answered her cell phone, I took a deep breath.

"Hey, mom, it's me on Jasmine's phone. I'm okay, but I'm at Hawthorne Park and I need you to come get me. The police are here...and someone else I think you're going to be surprised to see."

17

A Hairy Situation

My mom pulled up and rushed across the street toward the park. She looked pale and frantic until she caught sight of me. The relief which washed over her face was almost immediately replaced with rage at the sight of Clifton Blake.

"You!" She stalked across the sidewalk toward us, her fists balled at her side. "What are you doing here?"

Clifton Blake took a step back and Officer Barnes took a step forward, her hand up to stop mom in her tracks.

"Ma'am."

Mom put her hands on her hips, her mouth tight. "Would somebody like to tell me what's going on here?"

"We received a call from this young lady—" Officer Barnes indicated Jasmine.

"I'm Jasmine," she said to Mom, touching her fingertips to her chest.

Mom nodded but didn't give her usual warm smile when being introduced to someone.

"Apparently the children had ventured into the woods behind the park to collect samples for a science project."

Officer Mustache grunted his skepticism, but Officer Barnes continued as if he hadn't made a sound.

"They were frightened because of an encounter they experienced while deep in the woods. When we investigated, we found this man who claims to be the boy's father."

Mom inhaled sharply and turned to me. Her eyes were pleading, begging me not to be angry with her. "Well, I guess the cat is out of the bag. Jake, this is your father, Clifton Blake."

"We've met." I kept my face as unemotional as possible.

"Baby," she began, but stopped when she couldn't find the words to say to me after a lifetime of keeping me separated from the man standing in front of us.

"Hello, Bianca."

"Hi, Cliff."

I stood motionless, fascinated by their exchange, by the tension which existed between them like crackling power lines, by the mind-blowing realization I stood in the midst of both my parents for the first time since I'd been a newborn.

A squawk came over the radios, which were attached to the belts of Officer Barnes and the Mustache. A clipped voice rattled off various codes and an address.

"That's us. Will you all be okay here if we leave?" Officer Barnes made eye contact with each of us.

We all reassured her with head nods and my mother said "Of course," which seemed to make Barnes feel better about the situation.

I turned to Jasmine. "What about you? Can your parents come get you?"

"I texted my mom but haven't heard from her yet. I can call an Uber or a Lyft."

"Nonsense," my mother said. "I'll give you a ride."

With that, Officer Barnes and the Mustache bid us farewell and headed to their squad car. The rest of us were silent for several moments, no one quite sure what to say next.

Finally, my mom sighed and said, "Well, it seems as though we've got a lot to talk about. Cliff, meet Jake and me at my dad's. Jasmine, we'll drop you on the way."

When we arrived at my grandfather's house, an unfamiliar black car was already parked in the driveway. My mom hadn't said much on the drive home, but she put her hand on mine as I started to reach over and unbuckle my seatbelt.

"I'm sure I'm not your favorite person right now." Her voice sounded small and timid.

"You're right."

I glanced at her and saw how sad and worried she was. My stomach dropped.

"I'm not mad…okay, I am mad. I'm trying not to be, but…"

"It's okay. You have every right to be mad."

"Mostly I'm just frustrated and confused and hurt. I knew about the letter, and I asked Gramps about it—"

"You saw the letter? And Gramps knew you knew about it? Why didn't either of you come to me?" Her eyebrows pulled together in hurt and confusion. There was a lot of that going around.

"I came across it in the stack sitting on the kitchen counter. I didn't ask you about it because I didn't know how to feel. I love you, Mom. You're the most important person in the entire world to me. I know you would never do anything you thought might hurt me. I believe you thought you were acting in my best interest, but it did hurt, knowing my father wanted to see me and not only did you refuse, you kept the truth from me. My whole life I've wondered about this man…about who he was, what he looked like, and why he didn't want to know me. So, when I realized that wasn't the case and he did want to know me, I had lots of feelings about it. I hadn't quite sorted out those feelings enough to talk to you yet, but now he's here, and it's time to get it all out on the table. All of it. The good, the bad, and the ugly."

Mom's mouth wriggled like she was trying not to cry. She gave one head nod and released my hand. "You're becoming quite the mature young man, Jakey."

When we walked into the house, Clifton Blake had taken a seat on the couch across from Gramps, who sat in his old recliner by the fireplace. Gramps wore a wary expression.

I sat in the recliner opposite Gramps, forcing my mother to either sit on the floor or on the couch next to Clifton. She eased her way onto the sofa cushion as if it were a board of nails. I got a twisted bit of satisfaction watching her squirm. I didn't want to hurt her, but she deserved to be a little uncomfortable, considering the circumstances.

There were many glances exchanged among all of us before Gramps broke the ice. "Jake, how are you feeling? This has got to be a big shock."

"Ya think?"

"Jake!" my mother scolded. "Don't be rude to your grandfather."

Gramps reached out to her as if to say *it's okay.* "Bianca, it's perfectly understandable for Jake to be angry right now, with all of us. We're the grown-ups in his life, and we've let him down."

"I tried to explain to him it wasn't your fault. I was a disaster back then. I was selfish and self-destructive, and I don't blame you for keeping him from me."

My mom nodded her head curtly. It annoyed me

that Clifton Blake was defending my mother. I wanted him to be on my side. I was the wronged party here.

"I've changed, Bianca. I've turned my life around, and I've already missed so much of his childhood. I just want a chance to prove I'm not the same man I used to be."

He looked so earnest I felt my heart skip a beat. So, this was what it felt like to be wanted by your father.

"What exactly are you looking for out of this situation? And what are you willing to give?" Mom crossed her arms over her chest and side-eyed him.

I wanted to know the answers to those questions also.

"I'm willing to relocate to the area. I've already talked to my father about opening a hotel in Seattle. For the past several years I've been learning the ropes of his company and he's willing to give me a shot at running my own place. I'm financially stable now, so I'm able catch you up on back child support and begin making monthly payments. You'll be able to get a place of your own."

"I like living with Gramps!" I glanced over at my grandfather who looked pleasantly surprised at my outburst.

Clifton Blake held out his palms in surrender. "Whoa! I just meant you'd be able to, not that you'd have to do so."

Mom's eyebrow arched. "You have yet to tell me what you want in return."

"I wanna see my kid on a regular basis. We can formalize an agreement if you'd like, but I'm simply grateful for any time I'll get to spend with him."

Mom looked at Gramps, whose face was unreadable. Then she looked at me. I'm not sure what she saw in my expression, but hers softened and became a little sad again. She turned back to the man sitting next to her.

"I'm guess okay with you spending time with Jake, starting on a probationary basis."

"What does that mean?"

I knew I'd heard the word before, in relation to people who were in trouble. Like, instead of being sent to jail, a person might have been put on probation instead.

"It means as long as I respect your mom's rules, and as long as I do what I say I'm gonna do, show up when I say I will, pay money as promised, we can spend time together. Would you like spending time together, son, so we can get to know each other?"

"Of course I would! I've been waiting for this my whole life!"

I looked over at my mom and she smiled, but a tear had formed in the corner of her eye. I couldn't tell if it was a happy tear or a sad tear. It would make sense if it were a sad tear. After all, she'd had me to herself since the day I was born. I hoped, though, it was a happy tear because I felt happy. I looked back and forth between my mother and my father, and then I pinched myself because I couldn't believe it was actually happening.

"Bianca, how would you feel about me taking Jake out for about an hour to talk and get to known each other? I can have him back before dinner. Maybe he'll tell me what he was really doing in those woods today."

And then my father winked at me for the very first time.

18

You Scream, I Scream, We All Scream for Sasquatch Chip Ice Cream

"What can I get you, hon?" The woman with big fluffy hair smiled at me.

"Oh, I, uh, can I have a scoop of Sasquatch Chip?"

"Sure thing." She began to scoop the chocolate ice cream with large chunks of chocolate.

"You sure you don't want two scoops? I feel like if there ever were a two-scoop kind of day, it would be this one." Clifton Blake winked at me for a second time.

"I'm not sure my mom would like that idea. She doesn't let me eat too much sugar and it's so close to dinnertime."

"Hey kid," the lady said. "It's not often I hear dads encouraging their kid to get a second scoop. If I were you, I'd go for it."

It felt strange hearing her call the man next to me my dad, even though it was true.

"I guess this one time."

He reached over and tousled my hair. I'd seen movies and shows where dads did stuff like that, but I'd never thought it would happen to me. As it turned out, I didn't really like having my hair mussed like a dog. I wasn't about to say anything to him about it, though. He was as new at this dad thing as I was.

After we got our ice cream, we sat at a booth. Both of us were really nervous. I wished my mom had been there, because she always knew what to say when things got awkward, but she'd somewhat reluctantly let us have some one-on-one father-son bonding time.

"I know I threw a lot at you when we were at the park. Do you have any questions for me?" He licked his ice cream cone.

I wanted to ask why he hadn't been in my life, but thought I would start with an easier question. "You said for you it was love at first sight, but for my mom it wasn't. So, how did you get her to go out with you?"

"I asked. A lot." He laughed. "I'm sure part of her reluctance was I had a reputation for…going on a lot of dates. But she was special, I knew it from the moment I met her. So, I didn't give up. Eventually, I got her to agree to one date. And then another. Pretty soon, we'd eloped at City Hall. We were inseparable. She was Chip, I was Dale. She was Tweedle-Dee, I was Tweedle-Dum…literally. Emphasis on the dum."

"You said you hurt her."

He nodded, his face heavy with sadness. "I made a lot of choices back then which hurt your mother very much. I'd lost my job because I acted irresponsible. I felt embarrassed and angry, and your mom was disappointed. Snow White had always been really flirty, and she offered to be a shoulder for me to cry on. I betrayed your mother at her most vulnerable time. Bianca—I mean, your mom—she'd found out she was pregnant with you and had planned to tell me that night. Instead, she got her heart broken."

I'd been so mad at my mom for keeping my dad from me, I hadn't thought about how hard it had been for her. Hearing his side of the story, I felt angry at him for making her feel so bad. Still, at the same time I really wanted to like him, and I was tired of being mad…at my mom, at Gramps. It didn't feel good. My thoughts and feelings were jumbled like when you first open a puzzle box and the pieces are mixed up.

"What happened next?" I asked.

"She filed for divorce right after we separated and I signed the papers right away, hoping once she'd cooled off, we could make a fresh start. I didn't hear from her for months, until she called to say she'd had a baby. I hadn't known she was pregnant. She never put me on your birth certificate."

I shook my head. "Just because you weren't a good husband, that didn't mean you shouldn't be my dad."

"I could have fought for you. I should have fought for you. Instead, after your mom and I broke up, things went from bad to worse for me. The truth is, I wasn't in any place to be a father. My own father had practically disowned me so I could barely support myself financially, much less a family. My head was kinda messed up, and I knew she was right to keep me away from you. I'll tell you all the details some time, but I'm not quite ready to today. Eventually I got my act together. I was busy trying to rebuild my life while she moved up the corporate ladder. Just about the time I was going to ask to see you, she notified me you were moving all the way across the country. I told her it was unacceptable, but she reminded me I wasn't on your birth certificate and had no established parental rights. She said she'd told me about the move out of courtesy, but you were still off-limits. I knew she'd originally come from this area, so I searched online records and found your grandfather. I tried to call but she ignored my voicemails. I sent a letter—"

"I saw it. I asked my grandfather about it, and he said it was my mother's choice."

"How did you feel about that?"

"Mad and hurt. I've wondered about you my whole life, but she wouldn't tell me anything. She only told me you were a big man in more ways than one."

Clifton Blake chuckled. "Really. Well, I guess she meant my height and my father."

"Your father?"

"My father is a hotel developer in Orlando and Kissimmee. He's active and well-known in the community, so I grew up in the spotlight with a lot of money and privilege. He got me a Disney World job because I wasn't showing a lot of self-motivation and he was golf buddies with a bigwig there. She probably meant those high-level connections. Of course, it didn't keep me from getting fired."

"Now you work for your father? And you're going to move here?"

"That's the plan."

He smiled at me, and my eyes filled with tears. My whole life I'd wanted to know my dad and have him look at me that way. It was more than I'd even imagined. Embarrassed and overwhelmed with emotion, I wiped my face with my sleeve and took a deep breath.

He cleared his throat. "So, uh, are you in the fifth grade?"

I was grateful for the change in subject. "Sixth. I'm short for my age."

"I'm not sure I'd know the difference between what fifth and sixth graders look like. I don't spend a lot of time around kids. Don't get too discouraged about being shorter than the other boys. I wasn't tall when I was your age. Then I hit high school and I grew about a foot over one summer. My mom started buying me shoes that were two sizes too big because I kept outgrowing the ones she'd just gotten."

"What size are you now?"

"Thirteen."

"Whoa! You really are big!"

Clifton Blake laughed at this. "So, what were you and your friend doing at the park today?"

I sat there licking my ice cream, battling whether I should tell him or not. What if I scared him off, and he didn't want to get to know me once he realized I had an unusual fascination with giant ape-men and sea monsters?

"Jake, you can tell me anything. I promise, I won't judge you."

I took a deep breath. "We were looking for Bigfoot."

He stopped licking his cone.

"I know. It sounds crazy. Jasmine, the girl you saw with me at the park, she hired me to investigate a sighting."

"Sasquatch Hunters of Washington, Inc." He nodded. "I found your flyer."

"So, it was you who called!"

"Someone had put up a flyer at the coffee shop. I saw your name, so I thought I'd see what it was all about. I figured you and your friends were just goofing around. The girl who answered, Jasmine, called herself co-president."

"Vice president. I'm the president."

"What about the squeaky voice I heard in the background?"

"That's Lanny. He's our executive assistant."

"I see."

"What I can't quite figure out is why you started throwing rocks at us."

Clifton looked straight into my eyes. "Jake, I promise you. I didn't throw anything at you. If someone threw rocks at you back in those woods, it certainly wasn't me."

• • •

Clifton dropped me off back at home with a belly full of ice cream and a promise to spend the day together on Saturday. My mother said it was fine. The spending Saturday together part. I didn't tell her about the belly full of ice cream.

After he left, she pulled me into the biggest tightest hug she'd ever given me.

"You know I love you more than anyone or anything in this whole entire world, don't you?"

"Mmm hmm."

She held me so tight I could barely speak.

"I'm so sorry about all this. I didn't mean to hurt you. I think sometimes I forget you're not a little boy anymore. You're nearly a teenager. You're smart, and thoughtful, and it's time I start letting you make some choices of your own. I know you'll make wise decisions, but even when you don't, even when you make mistakes, as we're all bound to do, I will always be here for you."

"I know, Mom. I love you."

"I love you more than you could possibly imagine."

"Mom?"

"Yes, baby?"

"Hug's. A little. Too. Tight."

She laughed and loosened her grip. "You may be growing up, but don't think I'm letting go of you all the way." She gave me one more squeeze for good measure. "Okay, let's go make dinner. I'm thinking chicken and broccoli cheesy casserole, your favorite."

Inwardly I groaned, my full stomach protesting. Outwardly I put on a big smile. "Sounds great!"

19

The Mahajan Film

On Friday night Jasmine and I arrived at Lanny's house at seven for popcorn and a viewing of the video taken by Lanny and his dad while flying a drone with a camera attached over the woods and the wetlands behind the park. The Mahajan home could only be described as warm. Warm colors blanketed the walls, warm smells hung in the air from dinner, and the thermostat had been set to about seventy-five degrees. Lanny's parents welcomed us with smiles so big it was easy to see where he'd gotten his enthusiastic personality.

I didn't know what I expected to see on the film. We

already had an explanation for what we'd encountered in the woods when my father had been dragged out in his yellow rain slicker by the police, but part of me wasn't completely convinced his presence explained everything experienced first by Jasmine and her friends Kayla, Danielle, and Erika, and then by the Sasquatch Hunters crew.

Clifton Blake hadn't even been in the state when Jasmine and the girls had their spooky incident.

When I'd gone for ice cream with Clifton…er…my dad (such a strange feeling to call anyone Dad, much less a guy I'd only just met), I'd sworn him to secrecy before I told him all about Gramps' story, being hired by Jasmine, and what had happened in our various investigations into the woods. He insisted again he hadn't thrown anything at us to scare us away, and from his hiding spot, he hadn't been able to see too much. When he heard the thump, he assumed we'd dropped something as we ran out. He'd bided his time near the entrance when Officer Barnes and the Mustache showed up, so he hadn't ventured very deep in the woods to see if anything or anyone else was in there.

He had no explanation for all these incidents, and his curiosity had been piqued, so he suggested maybe the two of us do a little Bigfoot hunting as well. I told him I had to check with my partners.

That's truly what Jasmine and Lanny were, partners. As much as I'd been resistant to the idea, it turned out I liked being a part of a team. There was still a hierarchy in our organization, but their input had become extremely important to me, and I felt grateful to have them.

The three of us settled in on the couch where bowls of popcorn were already popped and waiting for us on the coffee table. Lanny's dad fiddled with some cords behind the big screen TV, muttering about inputs and HDMI. Suddenly, a still shot of Lanny standing in the park came on and we all cheered.

I felt a lot of emotions in that moment: excitement and anticipation about what we might see, happiness I was there with my new friends, and a lingering hope for the future now my father was in my life.

I'd overcome a lot of tough things recently. I'd moved across the country away from everything and everyone I'd ever known—except Gramps and my mom—to start at a new school where I'd managed to get on the target list of one of the worst bullies I'd ever met, not to mention finding myself in the principal's office on my very first day. I'd discovered my mother had kept my father away from me and my grandfather had known about it.

On top of that, my theory about a Bigfoot in the woods across from Hawthorne Elementary was in serious jeopardy after discovering that my father had been skulking around, watching and observing me, and following us into the forest. It was possible much of what we'd experienced could be chalked up to him.

While a big part of my motivation for discovering a real-life Sasquatch had been to get enough attention for my dad to come find me, and that no longer applied, I still had other reasons to pursue it which were equally important.

I wanted to validate Gramps' story, so he wasn't just "Crazy Old Man Nelson" but someone who'd been lucky enough to come face to face with a legendary creature and lived to talk about it. I needed him to not be a fibber and I needed to know he wasn't making stuff up to entertain me, because if that were the case, I'd fallen for it and I didn't want to be a foolish little kid who believed in things that weren't real. It was also important for my relationship with Gramps to know I could trust what he said. The trust level between us had taken some hits recently, on both sides, and I really wanted to build it back again.

Mostly, I just wanted Sasquatch to exist. And the Loch Ness Monster. Maybe not chupacabras 'cause they were kinda gross and creepy, but there was something intriguing about the possibility that in the most remote parts of the world, whole species were hiding which had yet to be discovered. Maybe I didn't really want to prove the existence of cryptids, just get enough evidence they might exist to keep the mysteries alive. I'd recently realized the hunt was often better than the discovery itself.

As I looked to the left and right of me, Jasmine and Lanny's eyes were glued to the screen. The excitement on their faces mirrored what I felt. Like I said, I hadn't intended to partner with anyone, but here I was, and it felt really good to be sharing the journey with them. I felt lucky.

The beginning of the video contained a lot of footage of Lanny and his dad messing around with the drone, the camera, and the controller. The drone flew up quickly, and then drop even faster. Sometimes it would go in circles, and Lanny's dad would start running around holding out his arms to try and catch it before it hit the ground.

At one point it got stuck in a tall maple tree at the edge of the park. Lanny's dad hoisted him onto a branch so he could reach and grab it. The first few attempts were unsuccessful. He broke off a branch, handed it to Lanny, and lifted him back into the tree. After waving the stick around, its leaves brushing the remote-controlled plane but without impact, he finally jostled it loose and caught it on the way down before it could hit the ground.

"Nice job, Lanny!" I gave him a fist bump.

"Thanks! It was an ordeal, but we got it." His face beamed with pride.

"Pretty impressive," agreed Jasmine. "I don't think my brother would have been brave enough to climb so high."

"Your brother and I tend to keep our hangouts to PS4," Lanny whispered, nodding, hoping his parents wouldn't hear what he'd actually been up to when he was supposed to be outside getting fresh air.

"Here we go!" I held up my hands. "Shh."

Jasmine harrumphed at my shushing and crossed her arms but didn't say anything else. Lanny leaned forward and scanned the screen for any anomalies.

The drone glided above the pine trees, some of which were over a hundred feet tall. The experience, with the 70-inch TV screen and surround sound, reminded me of Disney World's Soarin' Around the World virtual flight simulator. All that we were missing was pine-scented spray to complete the multi-sensory experience.

Whoever had been controlling the drone tended to make a lot of swoops and dips, causing my stomach to feel funny and making my head a little dizzy. Most of the woods were pretty thick, but when the plane flew high you could see for miles around. In the distance to the west were the Olympic Mountains on the peninsula, while the Cascades towered over the valley to the east. The scene was breathtaking and exhilarating and I felt as if I myself were flying.

Curving to the west, away from the main road and deeper into the woods, the view was expansive. Ahead were the wetlands, more woods, and some lakes. One of the lakes had a dock extending into it from the shoreline. A strip of grass was lined by more pine trees as far as the eye—and drone—could see.

The camera began losing altitude, slowly descending toward the wetlands. A massive log lay on its side, likely a tree felled in a storm, as evidenced by the jagged stump adjacent to it. The log had jammed the flow of water, and, upon closer inspection, a heap of debris looked to be a beaver dam. Sticks and leaves stacked upon each other to form a mound with water swirling around the barrier. There were a couple other mounds in various areas throughout the wetlands, and a few other stumps and tree logs. In some areas, trees grew out of the swamp, indicating shallower ground. Portions of land jutted into the water, with thick shrubs leaving little space for anyone—or anything—to walk.

As the sun begin to sink behind the Olympics in the distance, so did my hopes of finding evidence of a Bigfoot living in the wetlands behind Hawthorne Park. The whir of the drone slowed, indicating the battery was getting low on juice and I couldn't help but feel a little drained of enthusiasm myself.

Lanny got up from the couch and stood between us and the TV with his hands on his hips. "Well, that was a bust. Sorry guys, I'd hoped this would be our Patterson-Gimlin Film." He was referring to the most famous Bigfoot recording of all time.

Jasmine yawned and stretched her arms above her head. "Well, it was still entertaining. I've never seen this area from above like that. It was pretty cool."

My shoulders slumped. "Yeah, it was still cool. Thanks, Lanny, and tell your parents thank you for letting us come over. I guess for now we're gonna have to give up on any hope of finding a Bigfoot in Hawthorne Park. I mean, it was a crazy ide—"

"What was that?" Jasmine interrupted, her eyes big, her head craning around Lanny to get a better look at the screen.

"What was what?" My heart picked up tempo just a bit.

"Lanny, where's the remote?" she asked. "You gotta rewind it a few seconds."

Lanny grabbed the remote off the coffee table and turned around to face the TV. "Tell me where you want me to stop."

The scenes flew past in rapid reverse.

"There!" Jasmine shouted. "Just at the edge!"

Lanny pressed play. None of us took even a breath as we waited for whatever Jasmine had seen to appear. The drone performed some acrobatics in the sky and the camera had turned upside down.

"Pause!" Jasmine shouted again.

The frame froze as if the drone were dangling, suspended in the air like a bat hanging from the rafters.

All three of us stood and moved closer to the screen. We tilted our heads far to the left in an attempt to look right-side-up at the video. Lanny was so contorted his head was level with his hips and he nearly fell over. All the blood in my body seemed to be pooling in my brain, causing me to feel lightheaded.

"What are we looking at?" Lanny's voice sounded garbled from his throat being bent like a kinked garden hose.

Jasmine's hair cascaded over her slanted face, causing her to have to constantly brush it out of her eyes so she could see. I thought she kind of looked like Rapunzel hanging her mane out of the tower window to the waiting prince below. My face got warm at the thought, which I quickly tried to banish from my mind. The good news was, I could explain my red face away without anyone thinking I was blushing because all of us had turned practically purple from hanging our heads upside down.

"See where the trees jut out in that one area where it looks like the swamp may be a little shallower? The murky green stuff seems thicker, and there's a lot more of that tree stump's roots showing."

"Yeah, I see it."

Lanny nodded, and the movement caused him to wobble. I wasn't sure how much longer he'd be able to hold his position without collapsing.

"Do you see the dark form just inside the tree line?"

Jasmine pointed at the part of the screen where she wanted us to direct our attention.

I could no longer hold my head sideways. My neck had started to ache. I stood upright, stretched my neck, and then tilted to the opposite side in hopes of getting a better glance. I relocated the area she'd described. I wished we could zoom in, as it was difficult to see anything too clearly from that distance. Then, I spotted the figure she'd been talking about.

"I do! I see it!"

Lanny whined. "Where? I can't see anything!"

Just inside the wooded area, a large dark figure seemed to be standing. I squinted at the screen, inching closer. Unfortunately, the closer I got, the blurrier the figure appeared. I stepped back and stared.

"Why did this catch your attention?" I asked Jasmine. "I mean, it's definitely in the ballpark in terms of size, shape and color, but it could just be a big bush."

Jasmine jerked upright. She had a gleam in her eye. "Gimme the remote, Lanny."

He obliged her without protest.

Jasmine pointed the remote toward the TV and triumphantly said, "Watch this!"

As the video began moving again, we focused on the dark figure. And then the unthinkable happened. It was unmistakable. The figure moved.

All the spit in my mouth instantly dried up. My heart thumped so fast and so loud I expected the other two to yell at me to knock it off and be quiet. My palms tingled, as did every hair on my head, arms, and legs. I couldn't believe my eyes.

What just moments ago had looked like a big shrub or tree stump seemed to lean against one of the tall pines, causing it to sway. And then, just a second later, it was gone.

One thing I knew for certain, bushes didn't just get up and walk away.

In Search of...
Sasquatch

The room was dead silent...and then it wasn't. We all started talking at once, giggling hysterically and babbling like we'd lost our minds.

"Did you see that?" Jasmine crowed. "I told you! I knew it!"

"I thought I had the eagle eye, Jasmine, but man! You really spotted that thing like a pro hunter." I nudged her shoulder.

We're gonna be rich!" Lanny yelled, shaking his balled fists excitedly, as if all the energy inside his little body was about to burst out.

"Hold your horses, there, Lanny. We need more evidence. All we've really got is a shadowy figure on a grainy video from far away." Jasmine, always the voice of reason.

"I agree with Jasmine. We're definitely onto something, though. This video was taken long before my dad showed up, so it couldn't be him. It could be a person and it could even be a bear. My neighbor said last year he spotted a bear crossing the street just a couple miles away. I believe, based on everything we've experienced, there's a squatch in those woods, but people are gonna need cold hard proof before they move him from myth to reality."

• • •

We ventured out the next three Saturday afternoons exploring the woods behind Hawthorne Park after I'd spent the mornings working around my grandfather's house to pay him back for his broken scope. Lanny's parents made him join the soccer team after they discovered he'd been playing Fortnight at his friends' houses instead of playing outside, so he had a game every Saturday morning. Jasmine joined us after finishing her weekly piano lesson.

By the time we made it to the park each week, we only had a couple hours to investigate before the autumn darkness descended upon the woods. Each time, it rained cats and dogs, so we bundled in slickers and rubber boots before venturing into the wet and muddy wilderness. We had no use for umbrellas, as they'd get caught on branches weaving through the trees and bushes.

Once, when we were alone, I asked Jasmine again about the secret she and her friends were keeping that had to do with me. Her cheeks got pink and she promised me that someday she'd tell me, but she wasn't ready yet. She looked so uncomfortable, I decided I could be patient for a little while longer.

After two hours or so of fruitless searching, we'd gather back at Jasmine's for a post-investigation recap and strategy session. Jasmine's mom made us hot cocoa with mini marshmallows and her dad would pop his head in every now and then to ask if we'd found Bigfoot yet. He thought it was hilarious, but Jasmine simply rolled her eyes and said, "Daaaaaad!"

Speaking of dads...mine officially relocated from Orlando to Hawthorne, much to the supposed annoyance of my mother. She acted like she could barely tolerate Clifton, but every once in a while, he'd say something funny and I'd catch her trying not to laugh. I wasn't getting my hopes up too much, only a little. I was thrilled, though, because now I had somebody to watch Star Wars with or eat double scoop ice cream cones, as long as I didn't tell my mom. I updated him during our weekly hangouts about what our latest investigations had uncovered, and he'd even come along on one of them. He wasn't used to Washington weather yet, but he was a good sport anyway.

Even though we had yet to get definitive proof a Sasquatch lived in the wetlands across from Hawthorne Elementary, I'd made two great friends and I felt pretty excited to see what adventures awaited us.

So, when a couple weeks later Jasmine's family invited the members of Sasquatch Hunters of Washington, Inc. and our families up to their cabin at Harriman Lake for the upcoming long weekend, I jumped at the chance.

"I've done a lot of research on Harriman Lake," I told Jasmine and Lanny. "That place is a hotbed of Bigfoot sightings over the years. In fact, there was one just this past summer."

"Plus, there's the treasure." Jasmine flipped her hair over her shoulder.

Lanny's eyes grew wide. "Treasure?"

"What are you talking about?"

"Oh, I thought everyone knew about the treasure. Some old dude wrote a poem that's supposed to lead to treasure hidden in the area. It's famous."

I felt a chill of excitement. "Maybe we can solve it!"

Jasmine scoffed. "Lots of people have tried over the years. No one's found it. We're just kids. If grown-ups can't find it, how could we?"

I gave her a smug smile. "If anybody can, we can."

Lanny put his hand out. Jasmine and I stared at him.

"Hands." He jerked his head to indicate for us to put our hands in.

Jasmine and I reached our arms toward his little fingers until they looked like the spokes of a wheel.

"To finding Bigfoot and the treasure!" Lanny shouted.

Jasmine and I exchanged glances, shrugged our shoulders, and repeated, "To finding Bigfoot and the treasure!"

ACKNOWLEDGEMENTS

Writing is often a solo endeavor, but birthing a book is a group project.

In 2013 my husband, Jeff, gifted me my own website and said, "Time to show the world what you've got." It's been quite the journey here, and I couldn't have made it without his love, support, and excellent writing advice such as, "just keep adding verys until you hit your word count," and "chapter 36: everything up until now was a lie." He's the best man I know, and my very very very best friend.

I'm thankful for my kids, who've provided me with boatloads of comedic material over the years. Someday I hope to be as talented a writer as my eldest daughter, Sydney. My son Nathan is the king of dropping one-liners at just the right moment. My daughter Zoe is the best storyteller I know. And Parker…his imagination knows no bounds. I hope I've made you half as proud as you all make me.

My earliest and most fervent fans, my parents Anne and Bill… thank you for always believing in me.

For my siblings Billy, Heidi, Shannon, and Colleen, who tolerated my precociousness as a child and now celebrate it in my adulthood. We lost our sister Heidi this year. She never held back from letting me know she was in my corner, and I know she's still cheering for me.

To my in-laws Jan and Jim Adams and Toni Jackson, thank you for all your love and support. For my father-in-law Glen Jackson, who we lost fifteen years ago and for whom Salt Creek was his special place, I hope I've honored you well.

Special shout out to Yolanda Simpson and Lisa Gunnels. You both are superstars, and you have my heart. Thanks for keeping me (mostly) sane.

To my extended family and friends, I don't know how I got so lucky. Even if I don't name you specifically, I hope you know how important you've been in my life.

My writing support system:

Holly MacNaughton, who talked me into publishing my first short story in her literary review and held my hand through my inaugural editing/critique experience.

Tory Hunter (whatever your real name is), thank you for all your help with landing my agent.

My writing sisters, alumni from Susan's Breen's group at New York Pitch 2019: you inspire me and challenge me, and you are a force for good in this crazy world. Thank you to Alicia Blando, Melissa deSa, Joani Elliott, Robyn Fisher, Geneva Kachman, Pia Kealy, Delphine Ledesma, Angelina Madison, Laura Malin, Marti Mattia, Lisa Rayner, Victoria Ashlee, Grishma Shah, and Maria Skytta.

My editor Sunita Apte, thank you for believing in this series, my characters, and my writing. I'm thrilled to be part of the Reycraft family.

My agent Dawn Dowdle, thank you for taking a chance on me and all you've done to help me birth these book babies!

Finally, my beta reader extraordinaire, Ayushi Thakkar. I can't wait for the day you write your own books!

ABOUT THE AUTHOR

K.B. Jackson lives with her family in the Pacific Northwest. A full-time writer and part-time genealogist, she loves to craft stories with elements of history and family dynamics. She modeled the character of Jake after her youngest son, now a teenager, who has been fascinated by cryptids since kindergarten.